Lyd

&

The Annals of Veena

By

T. K. Jenkins

Copyright © 2022 T. K. Jenkins

ISBN: 9798799074432

All rights reserved, including the right to reproduce this book, or portions thereof in any form. No part of this text may be reproduced, transmitted, downloaded, decompiled, reverse engineered, or stored, in any form or introduced into any information storage and retrieval system, in any form or by any means, whether electronic or mechanical without the express written permission of the author.

This is a work of fiction. Names and characters are the product of the author's imagination and any resemblance to actual persons, living or dead, is entirely coincidental.

The views expressed in this work are solely those of the author and do not necessarily reflect the views of the publisher, and the publisher hereby disclaims any responsibility for them.

www.publishnation.co.uk

Chapter 1

Roselee House

Lydia stifled a yawn: she'd had a dreadful night's sleep. *What a truly terrible nightmare that was*, she thought to herself, relieved to have woken from her sleep. She tried to shrug off the memory of her bad dream and focused instead on what she would be doing on that summer morning.

Lydia gazed out of her bedroom window to check on the morning weather and found not a cloud in the summer sky. She could see, from the large, muntin-style window, the sea and the cove that she would explore practically every day. She looked across the field to St Cein's Church, with its prominent spire, from which the bells rang out the hour over the parish. And there was the majestic Gwendonia Castle, its never-ending battlements, round tower, and fairy-tale turrets looking as picturesque as ever. The castle was the home of Lady Adela Ronan, and was where Lydia's father and grandfather had worked for many years.

Lydia was the youngest in her family and she was a vibrant girl with the world at her feet: slight yet tall, with long, wavy, chestnut-brown hair and emerald-green eyes. Lydia's brother Ellis was two years older; a rather sophisticated yet sarcastic individual, with jet-black hair and bright, ocean-blue eyes.

Lydia and Ellis were close, but often failed to see eye to eye. Lydia resembled her mother and grandmother in their younger years in looks, but her inquisitiveness and adventurous nature came from Grandad.

Clank, Clank, clank! The noise of plates, pots, and pans echoed around Lydia's bedroom from the kitchen below, where her mother and grandmother were preparing breakfast. 'Lydia, Lydia! Breakfast is ready!' called her mother.

1

'OK, Mum, I'm coming! Lydia ran out of her bedroom and jumped down the stairs two steps at a time: *thud . . . thud . . . thud*!

'Will you stop jumping down those stairs at once!' yelled Mum.

She reached the bottom of the staircase and walked across the cold, tiled floor leading into the kitchen, where she joined Dad at the large, rustic table.

'Do you have something to say to your mother?' said Dad .

'Sorry,' Mum, for jumping down the stairs,' said Lydia pensively.

'That's OK,' Lydia, but will you please stop jumping down the staircase? I'm afraid that you'll end up hurting yourself,' Mum replied, while stirring something at the stove.

Dad leaned towards Lydia and whispered, 'Just slide down the banister, like I used to when I was young. She won't hear you then.'

'Thanks, Dad, I'll try that instead.' They giggled quietly together.

'Why do you always have to jump down the stairs? It's so stupid and childish,' said Ellis.

'Oh, be quiet for once mind your own business,' Lydia hissed.

'You two stop that arguing at once! You've only just gotten up and already you're starting to bicker,' said Gran sternly.

They both quickly apologised. 'Sorry, Gran.'

'I don't like it when you two argue. You are brother and sister for goodness' sake,' just stop it,' she continued.

'Look what you've done; you've upset Gran again,' Lydia mouthed at her brother.

Ellis glared back. 'Keep away from me! You're a pest.'

Lydia was furious. She placed both hands on the kitchen table and leaned forward, her face scowling, ready to respond, when suddenly Grandad came into the kitchen. 'Morning, everyone!' he beamed cheerily.

Lydia, unable to argue with Ellis further, dropped back down into her chair and folded her arms while continuing to frown at Ellis intensely.

'Morning, Grandad,' the children replied.

'Did you both sleep well?' he asked.

'Like a log,' replied Ellis.

'I didn't sleep well at all,' said Lydia, 'I had a terrible nightmare. There were people chasing me in the woods. It just felt like something dreadful was going to happen to me.'

Dad and Grandad reassured her. They told her that many children and adults have night terrors and not to worry about what she saw and felt.

'Be careful when you go to the pond—there'll be creatures after you there,' laughed Ellis.

'Dad, will you tell him to shut up? He's so horrible!' Lydia exclaimed.

'Don't be mean Ellis, you know Lydia always goes to the pond. She'll be frightened to go there now, so please apologise,' said Grandad.

'OK, OK, I'm sorry, it was only a joke,' said Ellis, sulking in his chair and glaring at Lydia for the telling-off.

'What will you do on this beautiful summer's day?' asked Gran, changing the subject.

Lydia told her that she was going to go to the cove, which was just a short distance away from their home, to collect pebbles for her arts and crafts projects.

Ellis could not understand why Lydia needed so many pebbles and shells: she collected them every time she went to the cove, and she went there nearly every day. 'You must have a tonne of them!' he said.

'If I had a tonne of pebbles and shells, why would I be collecting any more? Just keep your comments to yourself,' said Lydia.

'Whatever.'

'What about you, Ellis? What are your plans for the day?' Mum asked.

'Nothing. I haven't got any plans.'

'Go and keep your sister company, then.'

Ellis rolled his eyes. 'I'm not looking after her! She's always up to something, always wandering around—she'll be OK on her own.'

'I don't want you to come with me anyway. You're always moaning, and you can be so miserable at times!' said Lydia, angrily.

3

'That's enough! Both of you, or I'll ground you for a week!' cried Mum, exasperated.

'Now eat up before your breakfast gets cold, and no more arguing,' added Gran.

Finally, everyone was sitting down to breakfast. The kitchen door was wedged open, and a warm, gentle breeze flowed through and across Lydia's face. She couldn't wait for breakfast to finish so that she could make her way down to the cove.

The tranquillity of Lydia's breakfast was interrupted suddenly by a loud, crackling sound: it was Eggbert, Ellis's pet goose, flapping his wings as he waddled into the kitchen. Gran let out the most piercing scream, followed by Mum, who began screaming at the top of her lungs. 'Get him out! Get him out!' Both women began trying to shoo Eggbert out with tea towels, chasing him around and around the kitchen, but they couldn't catch him, as he was too fast. Lydia sat laughing and holding her stomach. She found the whole thing hilarious and quite forgot about the terrible nightmare she'd had.

'Will you stop laughing,' Lydia? You sound like a hyena. Come and help get him out of the kitchen!' said Mum, flustered.

'I'm sorry I can't, Mum! It's the funniest thing I've seen in ages,' laughed Lydia. 'This is your fault Ellis—you didn't close his pen properly, did you?' she guffawed.

'Be quiet!' snapped Ellis, who was looking slightly embarrassed.

Eventually, Dad managed to grab hold of Eggbert then took him out of the kitchen and put him back in his pen.

'Peace is restored once more!' laughed Grandad.

'That was so funny,' Lydia giggled.

'Yes, I'm sure we'll have many laughs telling this story in years to come,' said Grandad. 'So, Lydia, after you've been to the cove, are you looking forward to visiting Lady Ronan this afternoon?'

'Yes, I can't wait! I'll come home with you and Dad once you've both finished work. Can you wait for me?'

'Of course!'

'I'm sure you'll have a lovely time. Say hello to Lady Ronan for me,' said Mum.

'I will!' Lydia smiled.

4

Lydia, along with the rest of her family, had been visiting Lady Ronan in Gwendonia Castle since she was a little girl. Lady Ronan and Lydia were extremely fond of each other and Lydia always looked forward to the visits.

'Lydia, are you going to walk with us?' asked Grandad, as he took his flat cap off the hook and put it on his head, ready to walk to work. He had been the head gardener at Gwendonia for more than forty years, while Dad was the carpenter and handyman there.

'Yes, I'll walk with you. Can you wait a second? I need to get my bag.' Lydia ran to her bedroom, grabbed her bag, jumped back down the staircase and ran out of the front gate to where Dad and Grandad were waiting.

'I need my bag, you see, to collect pebbles,' she said, out of breath.

'Yes, we know,' they both laughed.

'You take that bag everywhere with you,' Dad added, with a smile.

'But it carries lots of things that I may need,' she replied.

Having made the walk across Roselee field they soon found themselves at the walled side entrance to the castle gardens. It was a large arched wooden door, with a cast-iron sign that said *Secret Garden*. Grandad fumbled in his trouser pocket and took out the key: it was a heavy, brown, old-looking metal key that made a loud clunking noise as the lock opened.

'Right Lydia, please don't be late for Lady Ronan this afternoon; you can easily lose track of time when you're on your adventures,' Dad smiled.

'I won't be late! I'll be here on time, I promise,' she called out as she began running down the path towards the cove.

'Be careful!' shouted Grandad.

'I will!' she yelled back, waving at them both.

As Lydia descended the cobbled path she met the local priest, Father David. 'Good morning, Lydia! Where are you off to in such a hurry? Ah, don't tell me—the cove?'

'Yes!' she laughed.

'Well, you have fun Lydia. I've got to sort out those church bells at St Cein's, and I hope that Mrs Sinclare has made me a batch of her Welsh cakes,' he chuckled as he headed to the church.

"Bye, Father David!' she shouted, before hurrying away, eager to be paddling in the sea. It was a picturesque walk along the stone path from the castle towards the cove. Windblown sand had accumulated and become trapped among the dense beach grasses, and wild coastal flowers were blooming all around.

Eventually, she came to a small stream that led down to the sea. She jumped on the steppingstones, stopping only to grab a small twig from the stream. Once on the beach, she took off her sandals and threw them into her bag and began wriggling her toes in the warm, soft sand. There was no one else at the cove around. *I have the cove all to myself,* she thought, gazing all around. She loved being alone on the beach as she explored, and collected pebbles, shells, and pieces of washed-up driftwood. She sat first on a large rock and began scraping her name into the wet sand with her twig, watching the waves break along the shoreline. She thought how fortunate she was to be living at Roselee House, in such peaceful and enchanting surroundings.

The local village was two miles away. Their closest neighbours were Lady Ronan, and Father David, who lived in a small cottage adjacent to St Cein's church.

The sun's rays bathed her face, arms, and legs with heat: it felt as though she were sitting in front of the log fire at Roselee House with a fleece wrapped around her, just like they did during the long, cold winters. She sat quietly for a while, looking pensively at the crystal-blue water and inhaling the aromatic sea air.

As she watched the gentle waves, Lydia's thoughts quickly returned to the terrifying nightmare that she'd had and she could not shake off the feeling that something awful was going to happen; a premonition, almost. She couldn't ever remember having had such a vivid dream before; one where people were calling and chasing her; where she knew instinctively that she had to run because if she didn't, she would be harmed.

She remembered, also, that in the dream she had hidden in a ruined abbey, among its moss-ridden stone walls. From her hiding place she'd seen a tall male with a grotesque face, surrounded by terrifying, eerie-looking men and women. The memory of it left Lydia feeling petrified and she tried not to think about it anymore.

After spending a considerable amount of time at the cove, Lydia set out on her walk back home along the magnificent coastline that stretched for miles and miles. She walked up the winding path where there were coastal flowers of every colour spread out like a giant floral carpet, as far as the eye could see.

Just past the stream, the path forked off towards Gwendonia's cobbled path. On her approach to the castle, Lydia saw Lady Ronan standing in the grand window, waving at her. Lydia began smiling and waved back excitedly at the prospect of that afternoon's visit.

'I'm back!' Lydia yelled as she arrived home.

'We're in the living room!' shouted Mum.

Lydia chatted with Mum and Gran until it was time to get ready for her afternoon visit.

'You'd best go and get changed,' said Mum.

'Where's Ellis?' asked Lydia.

'He was in the garden feeding Eggbert and doing his chores.'

As Lydia made her way to the staircase, Ellis came in from the garden. 'Where are you off to?' he asked.

'I told you, I'm visiting Lady Ronan for afternoon tea. Does anyone listen to me?'

'Oh, very posh.'

'Will you just stop it Ellis.'

'Ask Lady R if can you bring home some cakes,' he teased.

'I'm not asking Lady Ronan if can I bring food home,' Ellis!'

'Why not?'

'Because it's rude that's why!'

Gran, flustered and mortified at the thought of Lydia asking Lady Ronan for cakes to bring home, said, 'And you, Ellis Rose, had better not ask anyone for food or cakes, do you understand?'

'Ok,' he laughed, 'I'm only joking, Gran.' He gave his grandmother a big kiss on her cheek.

'You're such a tease, my boy,' Gran smiled.

'Annoying, I'd call him,' said Lydia.

'Don't be jealous, just because I'm the funny one in the family!'

Lydia rolled her eyes at him. 'I'll see you all later,' she sighed, before slowly making her way to the castle.

She walked across the field, climbed over the wooden stile and followed a snaking path uphill. The sun shone through a canopy of trees, and here and there the smell of wild garlic wafted up to her nose. As she neared the castle she looked up at a humungous stone wall adorned with wild ivy that crept into its every crevice.

Finally, she found herself standing outside the secret garden door; she turned the old large metal round doorknob, walked through, and followed a long gravel path. Eventually, she could hear Dad and Grandad talking.

'Ah, Lydia, you're on time,' said Grandad.

'Of course, I told you I wouldn't be late, didn't I?'

'Yes, you did. I bet you can't wait to taste those delicious cakes, can you?' Grandad giggled as tended the garden.

'Cook has been baking all morning—you can smell the cakes all the way out here in the garden. It's making my mouth water,' said Dad.

Dad pointed to a wooden bench he had finished. 'Well, Lydia, what do you think?' It was a memorial bench for his late friend, Edward, Lady Ronan's son, who had died many, many years before.

'It's wonderful, Dad,' she murmured, running her fingertips over the carvings. 'You're so clever. Lady Ronan will love it.'

'Do you really think so?'

'Dad, she won't just like it; she'll love it—your friend would love it too,' she said with a smile.

'Thank you, Lydia, it's taken me a very long time to make. I wanted to make it perfect for him. Go on, Lydia, sit on it; you'll be the first one,' he said excitedly.

'Can I? Don't you want to be the first one to try it out after all your hard work?'

'No, you can have the honour,' he smiled.

Lydia sat on the bench. It was surprisingly comfy for a wooden bench. Dad had carved the words *Gwendonia Castle* into its backrest, along with figures of Edward and him as children playing on the battlements. It was the loveliest memorial Lydia had ever seen.

'Come on, Dad, sit next to me; it's rather comfy.' Dad sat on the bench and for a moment they sat quietly together, admiring the beauty surrounding them.

'Here Lydia,' called out Grandad, holding up the most delightful flower posy in his hand, full of roses that he had just cut from the garden. 'Take this—it's for you to give to Lady Ronan.'

'Oh, Grandad, it's lovely,' said Lydia, as she nestled her face among the roses and inhaled their sweet scent.

'They're her favourite flower,' said Grandad.

'They're mine too, thank you, Grandad.'

'Right, it's time for you to go inside.'

'Ok, Grandad, I'm going, but can I walk through the labyrinth maze first?'

'Well, go on then, but you only have five minutes—not a minute longer,' he smiled.

Lydia entered the large maze, just as she had done numerous times before. She ran through its many twists and turns, eventually finding herself looking up at two marble cherub statues standing on large, white marble plinths.

'There you are, found you!' She had made it to the centre of the maze and knew she had to find her way back and quickly. 'I'm here! I'm here!' she called out breathlessly to her Grandad and Dad, who both laughed.

'Did you get to the centre?' Grandad asked.

'Yes, and I saw the statues,' she replied, hands on knees as she tried to catch her breath.

'Did they talk to you?' asked Grandad.

'Talk? Talk? What do you mean? They're statues, they can't talk!' exclaimed Lydia.

'Well, I've heard them talking when I have been tending the gardens,' he laughed.

'No, no, you haven't, Grandad, you're just teasing me,' she laughed.

'Stop it, Dad,' intervened Lydia's father. 'She'll never go in the maze again if you keep telling her stories like that.'

'Wouldn't it be great if they did come alive, Dad?' said Lydia.

'Well, I, for one, would be totally freaked out, and I'm certain Grandad would be too,' he said, laughing.

9

'Go, go, you must hurry,' said Dad.

'I'm going; I'll meet you here later,' Lydia called out as she quickly made her way through the ornamental gardens. Soon she was standing outside the castle's big kitchen door, eager for her visit.

Chapter 2

The Asiras

The castle kitchen door was wedged open with a cast-iron doorstop in the shape of a small sheep. *Gran would like that, for Roselee House*, Lydia chuckled to herself.

She popped her head into the vast kitchen, where she saw the kitchen staff engaging in lively chatter. *It's a bustling kitchen indeed*, she thought. Lydia saw silver platters of pastries, finger sandwiches, and mini Victoria sponges all laid out on the kitchen worktops. The aroma of the cakes was making Lydia's mouth water.

'Ahh Lydia, there you are, and you're on time—good girl,' said Cook, smiling. 'Are you looking forward to your visit today with Lady Ronan?'

'Yes, I am Mrs Clayton, thank you.'

'Oh, you needn't call me Mrs Clayton; I'm known as Cook around here, so you can call me Cook too,' she chuckled.

'OK, if you are sure about me calling you Cook,' said Lydia, sounding hesitant. 'I'm certain,' Cook said with a smile. She was such a pleasant, smiling, jolly woman.

'I've just finished baking and getting everything prepared, but I'll take you through to Lady Ronan. She really is looking forward to seeing you today,' said Cook. 'Come on, follow me; otherwise you'll get lost,' she laughed. 'You know Lydia, I have worked here for many years, way before you were born, and there are places and rooms within this castle that I've never seen, can you believe that? Gwendonia— it's just a marvellous place,' sighed Cook, who seemed very content to be working there.

'It is rather an enormous castle in all fairness,' Lydia replied.

'It really is, isn't it?' said Cook, chuckling.

Lydia followed Cook through several doors and passages until they came to the grand hallway. They walked across the gleaming marble floor, with not a speck of dirt to be seen, Cook's footsteps echoing throughout the hallway as the heels of her shoes clicked on the marble.

Although Lydia had been visiting Gwendonia since she was a small child, she had never been in this part of the castle before, and she had never before seen anything as palatial. She saw an enormous crystal chandelier hanging in the centre of the vast hallway, and admired the huge, colourful, stained-glass windows as the sun shone through them and bounced rainbow hues off the chandelier's crystals. It looked as though millions of fireflies were dancing above her: it was truly mesmerising.

Two life-size white marble statues, of a Greek god and goddess, stood on either side of the grand staircase. 'They look so human, don't they?' said Lydia.

'Yes, they do, and I'm telling you, Lydia, they have scared me on more than one occasion; they've definitely made me jump when I've locked up this part of the castle at night,' Cook laughed. 'Up we go then, this way.' They headed up the stairs.

The ruby-red stair carpet felt thick and luxurious: *It's like walking on a sponge*, thought Lydia. The carpet was held in place on every step by a thick brass stair rod. 'Aren't these lovely,' Lydia commented.

'I suppose they are, but they're a pain to clean and there's so many of them!' Cook laughed.

As Lydia followed her up the vast staircase, she noticed lots of cherubs had been carved into the balustrade, with the most beautiful, round faces, little wings, and baby-like, chubby short legs. *There are so many of them! Lady Ronan must like cherubs*, thought Lydia.

The staircase split off in two directions towards the top, and Cook and Lydia took the left side that led up to a long passageway. Lydia looked up at the ceiling and noticed more cherubs carved into the antique cornice. At that moment, she thought she saw one of them move. She rubbed both her eyes.

'You OK dear?' asked Cook.

'Yes, I think I may have a little sand in my eye from being down the cove earlier, that's all,' said Lydia. 'They're everywhere!' she blurted out.

'What did you say?'

'Cherubs. They're on the staircase, they're in the cornice, simply everywhere,' said Lydia.

'Yes, you've noticed them then. They're all around the castle. If you look for them, you'll see them, but aren't they sweet?' said Cook.

Lydia remained deep in thought as she followed Cook, trying to be rational about the cherub moving. *But how can carvings move? I sound completely mad!* she thought.

Mrs Clayton was knocking on the door of the sitting room.

'Come in!' called Lady Ronan.

'Lydia is here to see you, Lady Ronan,' said Cook.

'Ah, do come in Lydia—thank you, Mrs Clayton. Can you serve tea in fifteen minutes?'

'Yes, Lady Ronan,' said Cook, leaving the room and closing the door behind her.

'Hello Lady Ronan, thank you for inviting me to have afternoon tea with you! I'm so looking forward to it,' said Lydia.

'Me too,' Lady Ronan replied, 'Come and sit here. It's the most spectacular view; it's my favourite place, as you can see the sea for miles.'

Lady Ronan was the manifestation of elegance. She was a tall and lean woman, aged around 75, although nobody knew her exact age, as she would never reveal it to others. She had thick grey hair, slicked back into a high bun on her head. Lady Ronan always dressed as though she was attending a special occasion and on that day, she was wearing a cherry-red dress pinched in at the waist. The dress was adorned with a brooch, in the shape of a turtle coloured with bright glimmering turquoise gemstones, and pearl earrings dangled from Lady Ronan's ears.

They sat together at the window seat on a soft cushion embroidered with flowers and gazed through the Gothic window at the shimmering sun. A gentle summer breeze rippled the water of the lake below; and it looked like rows of diamond necklaces spread across an ocean.

'I often see you Lydia, when you are coming back from the cove. I was like you when I was young . . . you are *so* much like me, I was always exploring and spending time at the cove, looking for something magical to happen, or for lost treasure.'

'Oh, I never find any treasure,' sighed Lydia.

13

'Treasure is closer than you think.' Lady Ronan smiled mysteriously.

'What do you mean, Lady Ronan?'

'You'll find out soon enough. My, these roses are glorious.' She was admiring the roses that Lydia brought her from the garden.

'But what will I find out?'

There was a sharp knock on the door; it was Cook, bringing the afternoon tea. She placed the china cake stand full of finger sandwiches, pastries, and a selection of cakes onto a table draped in a crisp, white linen tablecloth, followed by some fine china crockery and freshly pressed linen napkins.

'Thank you, Mrs Clayton,' said Lady Ronan, as Cook nodded and quietly left the room.

'Go on, help yourself, Lydia,' Lady Ronan said, while she poured herself tea and began to sip from her china teacup. 'Cook made this especially for you; I know that Victoria sponge is your favourite.'

'It's lovely,' Lydia said with a full mouth, her lips covered in buttercream and strawberry jam, which she quickly wiped with a napkin.

'If you like it that much, I'll ask cook to put the remaining cakes in a tin so you can take them home to share with your family,' said Lady Ronan.

'Thank you, Lady Ronan that's very kind of you.'

They talked and talked about pretty much everything during the afternoon; Lady Ronan telling Lydia more tales of her time at Gwendonia . . . though not every tale.

'I see you most days sitting here, in the window seat, when I'm coming back from the cove. I always wave to you—do you always see me?' asked Lydia.

'Yes, I always see you. You're always smiling and waving to me.' Lady Ronan said she always knew it was Lydia because of her long hair blowing in the wind and by the rainbow-coloured duffle bag dangling by her side.

'I take it everywhere I go,' Lydia grinned.

Lady Ronan chuckled. 'What do you keep in there?'

'Shells, pebbles, and pieces of driftwood: any bits that have washed up onto the sand, really. I make art out of them. I'll make something for you, if you'd like.'

'I'd like that very much.'

'It won't be as good as your portraits and paintings hanging in the castle,' said Lydia, gazing at the splendour on display.

'True, I have been very fortunate in my life. However, I have also faced many unbearable and painful times, too,' said Lady Ronan. 'Can I tell you something,' Lydia?'

'Of course,' replied Lydia.

'While it's a privilege to attain and have wealth, you must always help others less fortunate than yourself. What you do with that wealth is important. When I was young, my grandmother would say, "Adela, we come into this world with nothing, and we leave this world with nothing but a good soul." So, in the pockets of time we have, we need to always help others. This is what makes us who we are: the need to be better people.'

'Your grandmother sounded like a wise lady.'

'She was. You would have liked her, Lydia. Now, more pastries?'

As they ate and talked, Lydia found herself distracted by the large, gold gilt mirror above the fireplace. It had three cherubs carved into the frame. They moved. They were talking to each other. *I must be going mad! Why do I see cherubs move all the time?*

'Is everything all right Lydia?' asked Lady Ronan.

'Yes, yes, I'm fine, thank you. I think I may be a little tired. I thought I saw the cherubs on your mirror moving. And talking to each other.'

'Really?' said Lady Ronan, not looking shocked in the slightest.

Embarrassed, Lydia continued, 'I've only just noticed, really, that there are an awful lot of cherubs here.'

'Yes! I just love cherubs—do you?'

'Yes, but why so many?'

Lady Ronan sipped her tea slowly. Finally, she put down her cup and stared at Lydia with an intense but kindly expression. 'Gwendonia is full of wonders and mystery and steeped in

15

ancient tales of bygone times. There is something extraordinary and enchanting about this place. As you will soon find out.'

Lydia frowned. *What was happening?*

'You are a very dear child and very special. You are brave and kind and strong—qualities that are most necessary in life. There will be times when you will need them all.'

Lydia was now full of cake, troubled by the gossiping cherubs, and thoroughly mystified by Lady Ronan's words. 'Why will I need to be brave and strong? I don't understand . . .'

'I want to give you something,' said Lady Ronan. She stood and, with some difficulty, walked across the room to her writing desk. She opened a creaky draw, took out a small, royal-blue velvet box and brought it back with her to her window seat.

'You must promise me that you will always keep this close to you. Never lose it. You must never lose it, promise me.' She handed the box to Lydia.

Lydia lifted the velvet lid. Inside, there was an oval shaped-transparent stone containing three ivory angels: two females on either side of male angel placed in the centre of the stone. 'It's beautiful, but what is it?' asked Lydia.

'The Lamanya Stone,' said Lady Ronan. 'It's magic. It can warn you when danger is close by. Remember that, always.'

Lydia, rather surprised at Lady Ronan's words, stammered, 'I can't. Thank you, but I can't—'

'Take it. You will need it. It's your destiny. Everything will make sense, very soon.'

Lydia noticed, with a shock, that Lady Ronan's eyes had filled with tears.

Although she still didn't understand the significance of the gift, Lydia made a solemn promise. 'I will always keep it safe, Lady Ronan, I promise. It'll be forever by my side.'

Lady Ronan placed her hand on Lydia's cheek and looked deep into her eyes. 'Keep safe and remember I'll always be with you. The cherubs you see are called the Asiras.'

'Where are you going? And what's an Asira?' Lydia asked, concerned that Lady Ronan was going to leave Gwendonia.

At that point, Lady Ronan's breathing became erratic, and she was finding it difficult to talk.

'Are you OK? Lady Ronan?' asked Lydia worriedly.

16

Lady Ronan collapsed onto the sitting room floor. Frantic, Lydia ran to the door. She began screaming down the passage. 'Help! Please help! Hurry! Hurry! It's Lady Ronan!' She nervously walked back into the room, tears rolling down her cheeks, and knelt on the floor beside Lady Ronan. She held her hand and told her that help was coming. Silent tears continued to stream down her face, while time appeared to stand still. There was an eerie silence in the room as Lydia waited for help to arrive.

The sitting room door burst open and several of Lady Ronan's staff ran into the room and surrounded their mistress, before lifting her onto a sofa. One servant ran for the doctor.

'What happened, Lydia?' asked Cook.

'We were talking, and Lady Ronan began struggling to breathe and then she collapsed on the floor. I just didn't know what to do.'

Lydia, visibly upset, was wringing her hands, unable to move and in shock, while staring down at Lady Ronan as she lay pale and silent on the sofa. She couldn't believe what she was witnessing, as the servants tried to revive Lady Ronan.

At that point, Dad and Grandad arrived in the room, anxious to know what had happened.

'Are you OK, Lydia?' Dad asked, his face full of concern. 'Come on, we need to take you home.'

'I can't! What about Lady Ronan? I need to stay with her, I need to make sure she'll be OK.'

'You're not staying Lydia, Lady Ronan is being cared for. The doctor has been called and he'll be here shortly,' said Dad. 'Come, Lydia, we need to go home.'

Lydia walked over to the table. There were half-eaten sandwiches and cakes, and cold tea in Lady Ronan's teacup. Lydia picked up the blue velvet box and quickly placed it in her pocket and walked back to her father.

He held her hand and began comforting her as they walked out of the sitting room.

'Will she be OK, Dad?'

'I don't know, is the honest answer,' he replied.

Lady Ronan's staff, visibly upset, remained in the sitting room, waiting for the doctor. As she left the room, Lydia looked over her shoulder at Lady Ronan. She silently thanked her for the Lamanya Stone and for being part of her life knowing that she would never see her again *Goodbye, Lady Ronan,* thought Lydia. 'She'll always be at Gwendonia; she will never leave, you know,' she said.

'Who? Who are you talking about, Lydia?' asked Dad.

'Lady Ronan.'

'That's a strange thing to say.'

'I don't think it's strange at all.'

Dad and Grandad looked at each other and told her that she was upset and in shock.

'Lydia, let's get you home to your mother and Grandma,' said Grandad.

'Not forgetting Ellis,' replied Dad.

'How can we possibly forget Ellis,' especially after the incident this morning with Eggbert.' Grandad said with a smile. Lydia managed a little smirk.

As they walked home in a sombre mood to Roselee House, Lydia had an overwhelming feeling that the day's events were only just the beginning of something important, and that everything was about to change.

Chapter 3

A Stranger in the Woods

Lady Ronan had died. Days had passed, but everyone in Roselee House was still upset and in shock. Lydia, especially, had taken her passing extremely hard and had spent most of the time since hearing the news in her bedroom.

Wanting to be alone, Lydia stared out of her bedroom window, from which she could see Gwendonia Castle, with tears gently rolling down her cheeks. As she wiped away her tears, she held the Lamanya Stone tightly in her hand.

There was a sudden but gentle knock on her bedroom door. 'Lydia, it's Mum. Please, can I come in?'

'Yes,' said Lydia, still staring out of her bedroom window.

'Are you OK?' asked Mum, while putting her both arms around her daughter. Lydia began sobbing into her arms.

'Why, Mum? Why did she have to die?' It'll never the be same again, ever.'

'I know it's hard, but she wouldn't want you to be crying and staying in your bedroom for days, would she?' her mother replied, 'She'd want you to be exploring down at the cove or having adventures at the pond.'

Lydia knew her mother was right and promised that she would venture out of the house the following day. Mum kissed her on her forehead, told her to call her if she needed anything and left the bedroom.

The summer sun was setting in the sky, setting it on fire with vibrant shades of pink, red, and orange, which lit up Gwendonia Castle. Bathed in the evening light, it resembled a mighty oil painting. Lydia looked towards the sky and hoped that Lady Ronan could see her standing in her bedroom window. She waved gently towards the sky, hoping that somehow, somewhere, Lady Ronan would be able to know how much she missed her. But as she did so, her face continued to stream with round, wet tears. They trickled down her face, ran past her nose and dripped off her chin onto her damp capped sleeved T-shirt.

Lydia continued to stare out of her bedroom window, now looking at St Cein's church. Her gaze then returned to the castle. *Why is there a light on in the round tower?* She gasped. With the passing of Lady Ronan, the castle would be deserted; or so it should have been.

Lydia hadn't noticed the light before, despite spending several days in her room staring out at Gwendonia. 'I'll tell Grandad in the morning,' she thought to herself, and settled down to go to sleep.

*

It was morning. Lydia made her way to the kitchen and sat next to Dad. 'Are you feeling better, Lydia?' he asked, concerned.

'I suppose so.'

'You've gone through a painful ordeal, and I know how upset you are; we all do. Everything will be all right. Lady Ronan will always be with you, you know, even if you can't actually see her.'

Lydia, sitting silently at the table, took comfort from what her father said. She began picking away at her breakfast, but didn't have much of an appetite. Ellis, who was sitting directly opposite her, mouthed, *Are you ok?* Lydia nodded and gave him a slight smile. *He's not his usual horrible and aggravating self,* she thought.

As the family sat around the kitchen table, Lydia's father talked about looking for another job, while Grandad was flustered about what should he do with the castle garden key. It was a distressing time for Lydia and the whole Rose family. Their future was uncertain; both Dad and Grandad were no longer needed at the castle, and out of work.

Lydia looked at the dangling garden key hanging on the hook. When breakfast had finished, she quickly took the key and shoved it into her pocket without anyone seeing. It was impulsive act and she knew that if her parents and grandparents knew that she had taken the key, she would be in big trouble. Still, she had an overwhelming need to return to the castle.

'I'm going out,' said Lydia.

'Do you want me to come with you?' asked Ellis.

'No, thank you, but thanks for offering.' She couldn't have her brother with her because she planned to trespass onto Gwendonia. If both were caught trespassing, they would have to accept the consequences. Lydia didn't want her brother to get into trouble.

'I'm so pleased that you are going out,' said Mum.

'Where are you going?' asked Grandad.

Her heart beating fast, Lydia said, 'Only to the cove and then to the pond, Grandad.'

She felt guilty that she had lied to him. She didn't dare tell him that aside from venturing to both the cove and the pond, she would be returning to the castle.

She made her way to the cove and collected a handful of shells. This time it felt even more personal because she would make pebble and shell art in the shape of Gwendonia. She looked out to sea then looked over her shoulder to the castle. It was eerily silent. *What's going to happen to you?* she thought, while an enormous wave of sadness came over her.

After a short while, she made her way back towards the castle, walking along the cobbled path which led to the garden entrance. Lydia stood outside the garden door and quickly rummaged through her bag, took out the key and held it in her hand and for a moment, staring at it. Then with a deep sigh and looking around to make sure that no one could see her, she turned the key in the lock. *Clunk!* The door was open. She quickly ran through, locking it behind her so that no one could follow her.

The garden was full of summer flowers in full bloom. She thought about the day Grandad had picked her roses to give to Lady Ronan.

She wandered around, admiring the grandeur of Gwendonia's gardens, knowing that she wasn't supposed to be there. Yet she felt peaceful in the castle grounds, even if she couldn't enter the majestic castle.

She sat on the memorial bench. By sitting quietly, she felt that she would make more memories, for she might never have another opportunity to visit the castle again. Life as Lydia had known it would never be the same again; it was as though she had returned to the castle to say her final goodbye.

Before she left the castle grounds, she decided to enter the labyrinth maze, and began walking its twists and turns. When she got to the middle, she could see that something was significantly different. 'Where have they gone?' she gasped, as she looked all around the centre of the maze.

The cherub statues were nowhere to be seen; only the plinths they had been standing on remained.

Lydia took a deep breath and walked back through the maze, thinking how irrational she was. 'Statues don't come to life, let alone talk,' she scoffed. She was back at the entrance: not a live walking statue in sight! *Maybe one of the staff has them?* she thought, but in truth, Lydia didn't have no idea where they'd gone.

Slowly, she walked down the gravel path and reluctantly put the key back into the lock: *clunk!* The door was open once more. She walked through the secret garden door and locked it firmly after her, believing that she had visited the castle for the last time.

As she crossed the field to Roselee House, she became nervous. What if Grandad knew that the key had gone missing?

'Ah, there you are,' the wanderer has returned! Where have you been?' Dad said, chuckling.

She didn't dare tell them she had been at the castle for over two hours! 'Oh, just down the cove, that's all. I passed Gwendonia. It's so quiet.'

'We all miss Gwendonia and Lady Ronan, but things will be much brighter soon, I'm sure,' said Dad, optimistically.

Curious, Lydia asked Grandad what he thought would happen to Gwendonia.

'I don't know, but I'm sure some nice family will buy it. Then you can make new friends. Now, wouldn't that be nice?'

'I suppose,' she replied sullenly. 'She didn't she have any relatives at all, though. Perhaps there might be some cousins?'

'I don't know . . . her husband died when her only son Edward was a small boy. Then he was killed in the war. What a dreadful time it was, just terrible.' Grandad sighed sadly.

'We grew up together,' Dad said. 'I would spend a lot of time at the castle and we were great friends. When he was 13 years old, he went to boarding school, somewhere in Oxford— England . . . Fitchet Hall, I think it was called. He always wanted to become an Army officer. When he'd return home for the holidays, we would meet up,' said Dad.

'Lady Ronan never wanted Edward to go away to boarding school. However, it was the most prestigious military boarding school and she always encouraged him to follow his dreams,' continued Grandad.

'Boarding school? I wouldn't like to go to boarding school; I'd miss going to the cove,' Lydia laughed.

'Many children attend boarding school and they enjoy it, but I suppose everyone is different,' said Grandad.

'Edward was in his early twenties, a young man with a bright future ahead of him, and then he died. His life was taken away from him too early. His passing had a terrible effect on Lady Ronan. She grieved for her beloved son until her very last breath, I'm sure,' said Dad.

After hearing about Edward, Lydia felt awful that she had not been honest, and couldn't wait to put the key back onto the hook.

'Are Mum and Gran back yet?' Lydia asked Grandad.

'Not yet,' he replied.

Lydia gave a sigh of relief when she realised that she could return the key without her mother and grandmother being in the kitchen. They had both gone into town for some groceries on their weekly day out. With time ticking away, she hurried into the house and went straight to the kitchen, took out the key from her bag and placed it back on the hook.

'What are you doing?' asked Ellis, who was peering around the doorway.

'Nothing, why?' said Lydia, flustered.

'Are you pinching the key for Gwendonia?' he giggled.

'Don't be so ridiculous! Why are you saying that? Why Ellis? Come on, why say that?' she persisted angrily.

'Will you calm down, Lydia! I was only messing around. I know you wouldn't take the key,' he said, and stormed off in a huff.

Lydia sat on the chair by the kitchen table, knowing that she had overreacted. She *had* taken the key and she had made him feel as though he had upset her. She felt an urgent need to apologise and shouted out his name. 'Ellis! Where are you? If you can hear me, I'm sorry, truly I am!'

23

'What are you sorry for?' asked Dad.

'Oh, Dad,' you startled me. I shouted at Ellis, it was my fault, so I'm apologising to him.'

'Good girl. If you know you're in the wrong, you must always be the bigger person and say sorry.'

'I don't think he's speaking to me now.'

Lydia's father reassured her that he would have a word with Ellis, and everything would be fine. 'Do you want to come and help Grandad and me weed the garden?'

'No thank you, Dad, I'm going for a walk to Sherrie's pond. I won't be long.'

Sherrie's pond was situated in the woods directly behind Roselee House. No one knew why it was called Sherrie's Pond, but it was a quiet, tranquil place. Lydia had been going to the pond as far back in her childhood as she could remember. She would walk to the pond with Dad. He would tell her many stories about his childhood, about nature, and they would pick blackberries together there.

'Only pick them from the centre of the bush, as the lower the blackberries are to the ground, the easier it is for the wildlife to wee on them!' Dad would continuously tell her. It was the same with the wild raspberry bushes. 'Only from the centre of the bush,' he'd repeat, which would make Lydia laugh.

She walked into the woods and took the same path to the pond as she had done hundreds of times before. This time she had the feeling, however, that someone or *something* was watching her. She put it down to what her brother had teased her about: her nightmare and the creatures that were in the woods. Wracked with the fear of someone watching her every move, she called out assertively. 'Who's there? I'll scream, and my father with hear me.' Suddenly, there was rustling in the bushes; a wild rabbit jumped out of the blackberry bushes. It startled Lydia, but she felt relieved that it was only a rabbit.

The pond was large and round and surrounded by tall trees and many colourful wildflowers, blooming in the tall grass. Besides the cove, it was a peaceful place to go paddling. It was a hot summer's day, so Lydia took off her sandals and dipped her toes, then her feet, into the cool pond water. With her hands cupped, she filled them with water and threw it over her face. It felt so refreshing. Sitting at the edge of the pond, her feet and face drying in the gleaming summer sun she could hear a noise in the distance, but coming closer: *Snap! Snap! Crack! Snap! Snap! Crack! Crack! Snap!* Someone was walking through the forest.

'Hello! Hello! Hello!' called out a male voice. Lydia jumped up quickly and was ready to run. 'Please, please don't be afraid! I've lost my way in the woods,' he laughed. 'I'm terribly sorry that I startled you; I thought I'd take a shortcut and lost my way as I haven't been back here for many years.' Lydia stared at the young man, wondering if she had ever seen him before.

'Do I know you?

'I don't believe so; what's your name?' he asked.

'Lydia Rose,' she replied with hesitation.

'That's a pretty name.'

'Thank you.'

'I used to come to the pond when I was young. Do you know these woods are enchanted with fairies, elves, and woodland creatures? They are all around,' the man said, looking around him.

'I don't think so, sorry, but your wrong. I never saw anything, and I've been here a thousand times. Fairies and elves!'' she scoffed.

'Just because you can't see them doesn't mean they're not real or not watching you. Many magical enchantments and strange happenings take place all around you that don't make any sense,' he replied.

Lydia didn't have a clue what the man was talking about and asked, 'Are you all right? Have you caught too much sun?'

'No, I'm fine, why do you ask?'

'I don't mean to be rude, but you're not making any sense, you know, talking about fairies being in the woods,' she said with a slight smile, hoping not to offend him.

'I understand that it sounds a little make-believe, but it's true. But what you must know is that there are also evil creatures that live in the woods,' he told her.

'I know what you are trying to do; you're trying to scare me, you're like my brother Ellis. He tries to scare me too,' she grinned. 'It's not working, I'm afraid.'

'I'm not trying to scare you, Lydia; I'm warning you that's all, just be on your guard at all times. You see, there is always good and bad in the world, like the fairies against the evil woodland creatures.'

Lydia looked at the stranger, thinking he was mad, but her thoughts turned to the nightmare she had had only days ago, of something chasing her through the forest. Maybe this man was not so mad after all; perhaps evil *was* lurking in the woods.

'Where are you going? Maybe I can help you find your way?' said Lydia.

'I'm heading to Gwendonia Castle.'

'Gwendonia?'

'Why yes, do you know of it?'

'Of course, I know where it is.'

'Then you can certainly help me get there. That's where Lady Adela Ronan lives. You know Lydia, I haven't been back for so many years; I can't wait to see the old girl! Is she still as wonderful as I remember?'

'Who are you referring to— the castle or Lady Ronan'?' asked Lydia, amused.

'Why, the castle of course,' he chuckled.

Lydia then had a flash of realisation that she would have to tell the stranger that Lady Ronan had died.

'Lady Ronan, do you know her?' asked the stranger.

'Yes, I did know her, but I'm afraid she passed away several days ago. I'm so sorry.'

Looking shocked, the man slumped onto the grass. 'Did you know her well?'

'Yes, I did. She was the loveliest lady; I miss her terribly.'

Lydia felt he was a kind soul, as he apologised for upsetting her.

'How did you know her? Are you a relative?' Lydia ventured.

'Yes,' you could say that.' he smiled.

'You may get to inherit the castle. Then my father and grandfather may keep their jobs, if you'll employ them,' she said excitedly, while trying to get all her words out coherently.

The man just smiled at Lydia and told her not to worry. 'All will be well; you'll see.

What are your father and grandfather's names?' he asked.

Lydia proudly told him that her dad was Daniel Rose, and that Grandad was John Rose. She told him that they had worked for Lady Ronan for years, but that they'd lost their jobs when she died. 'Maybe you could consider employing them if you get to own the castle?

'Lydia, will you stop worrying,' reiterated the stranger. 'If you don't mind, can you point me in the direction of Gwendonia?'

'Yes, sure, it's this way. I'll walk with you, as I need to get home,' said Lydia. 'But you're wasting your time, the castle is locked up, all the staff have left and it's completely empty.'

'I'll take a chance,' the stranger replied with a smile.

'There's my house, Roselee,' she said, pointing it out.

'I remember Roselee House, and your father Daniel,' he said, smiling.

'Do you want to come and say hello? My father would probably remember you,' she said excitedly.

'Maybe another time,' he replied.

'There she is!' Lydia exclaimed, pointing to the castle.

'It's lovely to be back and to see her again, and it was lovely meeting you also,' the stranger said.

'Yes, it was nice to meet you too. I do hope you'll inherit the castle!' Lydia shouted. 'What's your name again?'

He waved farwell as he crossed the field. 'I told you my name.'

'I don't think you did!' she yelled back.

He shouted something, but she couldn't make out what he was saying. She watched him until he was out of sight and quickly ran to tell Dad and Grandad about him.

'Dad, Grandad, Lady Ronan *does* have a relative, and he's walking to Gwendonia now,' she told them.

'What on earth are you talking about, Lydia?' asked Dad.

'I met a man in the woods,' she replied.

'You met a man in the woods?' he asked, raising his voice.

'Did he say anything bad, or hurt you?' quizzed Dad.

'No, dad, he was lovely, really.'

'Did he say he was a relative of Lady Ronan?' asked Dad impatiently.

27

'Well, not in those exact words—I asked him if he was a relative, and he said, "Yes you could say that". I think that's what he said,' she explained.

'What did he look like, Lydia?' asked Dad, concerned.

'Dark hair, about 6ft, oh, and he had blue eyes, and a dimple in his chin,' she told him. 'He said that he knew you and he hadn't been back for years.'

Both Lydia's father and grandfather looked at one another and asked Lydia the stranger's name. She explained he was shouting his name to her as he was walking across the field towards Gwendonia, but that she couldn't hear.

Lydia's father and grandfather told her to stay at Roselee while they made their way to Gwendonia to see if they could find the stranger.

After about an hour, Dad and Grandad returned home.

'Did you see him? Was he there? Dad, did you speak to him? Is he a relative?' Lydia continued to bombard Dad and Grandad with questions. But they had seen no one.

'He wasn't there? I don't understand,' she sighed, feeling disappointed.

'We walked around the castle perimeter, but there was no sign of him, there were no break-ins, nothing!' said Dad.

Where could he have gone? she thought, feeling puzzled by the events.

'If you see him again, get me at once, Lydia, do you understand?' said Dad sternly.

'Yes, Dad, I understand.'

'Maybe we'll meet him again, especially if he inherits the castle. I'm certain you'll get your jobs back,' she said optimistically.

'Lydia, I am quite certain, absolutely positive, that Lady Ronan did not have any relatives: none, in fact,' said Grandad emphatically.

'Then who could this stranger have been?'

'We don't know Lydia. That's why you need to come and tell us right away if you see him again. He could be anyone that knows that the castle is empty. There are a lot of valuables in that castle,' replied Dad.

Maybe he's a thief? And I helped him! I told him the castle was empty, she thought anxiously.

Lydia could not help but think of the stranger and their conversation about the enchanted woods. It was all very puzzling. *It must be nonsense*, thought Lydia. But who was this person? And what did he want?

It had been a long day, and once she had eaten, Lydia took herself off to her bedroom, exhausted. Before getting into bed, she looked out of her bedroom window and peered at Gwendonia from behind the curtain. The light was still on in the castle.

'Oh, no! The round tower light is still on; I forgot to tell Grandad.' Lydia quickly went downstairs to tell her grandfather. 'Come look, Grandad! It was on the night before too, but I forgot to tell you.'

Lydia went back to her bedroom, followed by Grandad. He went to the window and looked out towards Gwendonia.

'There's no light on in the round tower Lydia—come look for yourself.'

'Whatever do you mean? Let me look.' Grandad was right: there was no light on in the round tower. 'I don't understand, Grandad . . . I noticed it the past two nights, but now it's gone off!' she told him, looking completely baffled.

'Perhaps it's a reflection, or an optical illusion,' Grandad suggested.

Lydia felt wholeheartedly that it hadn't been an optical illusion but and actual electric light!

'Goodnight night, Lydia,' said Grandad, and left her bedroom.

While lying on her bed Lydia had an urge to look through her bedroom window again. She got up, opened her curtains and gasped. 'The lights are on again,' she said softly. She couldn't understand why the lights weren't on when Grandad had looked.

Lydia, curious as ever, quietly knocked Ellis's bedroom door. 'Ellis, please open your door,' she whispered.

Ellis answered. 'What are you doing up so late?'

She told him about the lights in the round tower and that their grandfather had looked out of her bedroom window, but had seen nothing.

'What's the big deal? So what?' said Ellis, looking confused.

29

'Don't you think it odd?'

'No, not really' said Ellis, not the slightest bit interested, 'Lydia, will you just go to bed.'

'I'm not leaving your bedroom until you have a look at the round tower,' she told him in a determined voice.

'For goodness' sake Lydia, I'll have a quick look, if it means you'll get out of my room.'

Ellis looked through his bedroom window. 'See? It's all in darkness, no lights on, Lydia, look for yourself,' he told her while huffing loudly.

Lydia looked out and it was the same as when Grandad had looked—no lights were on at the castle.

'OK, I'm going, but something really strange is happening and I don't know what,' she said.

'I know what's happening—all the deceased ancestors are having a party at the round tower,' Ellis chuckled, though realising his comments were insensitive, he apologised. 'I'm sorry for saying that: it wasn't a nice thing to say to you.' He felt terrible that he had made a joke at the most upsetting of times.

'I know you didn't mean it but think before you open your mouth in future,' said Lydia, returning to her bedroom and leaving Ellis feeling as if he had been told off by an adult.

Lydia was totally baffled as to why it was that only she could see the lights on at the castle. She knew that something wasn't quite right, but there was no chance of her ever returning to the castle to try to solve this mystery.

The following morning, Lydia's mother woke her, calling her from the bottom of the staircase. 'Lydia, Lydia! Will you come down, please?' She looked at the clock on her bedside table.

'I've missed breakfast! It's 9am!' The family always had breakfast between 7.30 and 8am. *Why didn't someone call me sooner?* she thought.

She rushed downstairs and looked for her mother, who was waving goodbye to the postman in the front garden.

'Mum, why didn't you call me for breakfast?

'I thought I'd let you have a lie-in this morning; you need to catch up on your sleep,' she smiled.

'I'm fine, really I am, but I'm starving.'

30

'Get yourself into the kitchen; your breakfast is ready for you,' replied her mother.

Lydia rushed into the kitchen and quickly began tucking into her breakfast.

Her mother glanced through the mail. 'Oh, look,' it's a letter addressed to you, but it's in the care of your father and me.'

'A letter for me?' said a shocked Lydia.

'Yes,' it's postmarked London,' replied Mum, handing Lydia the letter. 'Go on, open it,' she said, excitedly.

Lydia studied the envelope. 'You open it, mum,' she said, and passed the letter back to her mother, who opened it quickly and began reading:

Dear Mr & Mrs Rose,

It would be most appreciated if you could attend an appointment at Rubbelswick Chambers, London, on the 3rd of August at 12.30pm.

Your daughter Miss Lydia Rose's attendance will also be required, as this matter that relates to her specifically.

If the above date and time are not convenient, please do not hesitate to contact my secretary Mrs Everett on the telephone number below to make alternative arrangements.

I would, however, strongly advise that you make every effort to attend the appointment with me on the above date.

Yours sincerely,
Mr Ernest Rubbelswick QC

'There's got to be some sort of mistake,' said her mother, baffled. 'Daniel! Annie! John! Ellis! Come here! I need to show you something,' she shouted.

'What's a chamber?' asked Lydia.

'It's to do with the law, but I don't know exactly what it is. I think it's where solicitors work. This letter looks very important,' said Mum.

Lydia's family assembled in the living room, where her mother read out the letter once more. Everyone looked at one another, totally baffled by what they'd heard.

'There must be some mistake. I'll telephone them and sort this out,' said Dad.

He dialled the number and when it answered, he said, 'Hello, my name is Daniel Rose, and we've received a letter requesting we accompany our daughter to Rubbelswick offices in two days' time. I think there may be some mistake or typing error on your part?'

Lydia and her family were eager for Dad to finish the telephone call. The family stood around impatiently, waiting for him hang up.

'Well?' asked Lydia's mother eagerly.

'I don't know, Sarah. They wouldn't tell me over the telephone, but they said it is for us and that they need to see us in person.'

'Looks like we'll be travelling to London, Lydia,' said Dad, looking slightly puzzled. Lydia thought the family would be in trouble because she had trespassed on the castle grounds.

After some discussion, her curiosity outweighed all other thoughts. It was decided that Dad and Grandad would accompany Lydia to Rubbelswick Chambers, London, England.

Chapter 4

Rubbelswick Chambers

On 3rd August, Lydia, Dad and Grandad were all dressed in their finest attire, ready for their long journey to London. Even though Lydia was worried by the unexpected request from Rubbelswick Chambers, she was excited to be travelling to London. She had once travelled to Middlesex in England, to visit her cousin Grace, on many occasions, but had never had the opportunity to visit the city of London.

'Do you have everything for the journey?' asked Lydia's mother. 'Yes, Mum! I have my favourite book to read on the train, Gran has given me some sort of disgusting, and sickly sweets for me to suck on if I get travel sickness.'

'They're barley sugars,' her mother giggled, 'they're meant to cure travel sickness!'

'But even if I take them to stop the travel sickness, the sweets make me sick anyway, so there isn't any point in putting them in my mouth, is there?' Lydia laughed.

'Just keep them in your pocket. You know what Gran is like, she doesn't want you to get unwell. You know that Gran's mother— your great-grandmother—would give them to Gran when she travelled, so she swears by them.'

'I won't say anything to Gran about the sweets; I don't want to hurt her feelings.'

'Good girl!'

'Awe, Lydia, you look lovely in your pretty dress and shoes,' said Gran.

'Thanks, but I look six years old,' Lydia replied sarcastically. She didn't like the dress at all. She'd begged and pleaded with her mother to be allowed to wear something else instead of a dress, but Mum had told her no. 'Lydia, you are certainly not wearing anything else. You'll keep what you've got on, and I'll hear no more of it.'

'Who's this girl in our living room?' giggled Ellis. 'You're looking very pretty in your dress Lydia, like a little princess, you are.'

'Think you're funny, do you?' Lydia scowled.

'As a matter of fact, I do think I'm hilarious! I really wish I could take a photo of you,' he teased.

'Right, Princess Lydia, I'll see you tonight,' he laughed, as he left the room. Lydia was annoyed at her brother making fun of her dress and bellowed after him, 'Go and let Eggbert out of his pen again!'

But her mind returned again to the trip to London and the possible reason for being asked to Rubbelswick Chambers. Her thoughts were soon disrupted by Dad's voice. 'We'd best be off to catch the earlier train to Paddington, which will give us plenty of time to find our way to the chambers.'

Lydia, Dad, and Grandad climbed into the car for the journey to the local train station. As they were pulling off from outside Roselee House, Gran yelled, 'Stop! Stop! Take this, Lydia!' It was a linen bag.

'What's in here, Gran?' said Lydia, hoping it wasn't more barley sugars.

'Sandwiches—salmon and cucumber—some homemade Madeira cake, and a flask of milky coffee for your dad and Grandad, and a bottle of squash for you,' she beamed.

'We can buy food on the train!' said Grandad, 'You needn't have bothered making sandwiches for us Annie but thank you! You know how to look after us,' he smiled.

'We're actually going to London, Dad! We'll be able to see Big Ben, Trafalgar Square, and Buckingham Palace!' Lydia said excitedly.

'I don't think we'll have time to go sightseeing, I'm afraid. We have a tight schedule. You know we only have enough time to attend the appointment with Rubbelswick, and then we have to catch our train home,' said Dad.

'Ok,' said Lydia, who was very disappointed.

Grandad tried his utmost to cheer her up by saying that they would be able to see at least some of the tourist sights on the way to Rubbelswick's. Lydia beamed with delight on at the news.

After a short drive, they boarded the train and were heading for Paddington. 'It's a long journey,' sighed Lydia.

'I told you it would be,' didn't I?' said Dad.

'I didn't think it would take this long; we must have stopped a million times!'

'Don't worry Lydia, we're nearly in Paddington,' said Dad.

'It's taking forever,' Lydia sighed, her head gently pressed against the train window.

Suddenly, a voice boomed over the loudspeaker, *All stops to Paddington! All stops to Paddington!*

'Hooray! We are finally here,' she said, sarcastically.

'Just have a little patience,' Dad replied.

At last, they arrived in London and the Roses climbed off the train onto Platform 1. They had no idea where to find the exit. They tried to find their way through the crowds of people, who also seemed to have no idea where they were going.

The train station was very loud and chaotic. 'Come get your morning papers! Come get your morning papers!' a tall, gangly man bellowed from behind his kiosk. Lydia was utterly fascinated by all the activity and bustle around her. The place was nothing like she had ever seen before; a far cry away from the quaint seaside village she had left earlier that morning.

Finally, they found their way outside Paddington and Grandad quickly hailed a black London taxi. 'Where to mate?' the driver asked.

'Rubbelswick Chambers, Temple Avenue, if you'd be so kind,' Grandad replied.

'Oh, you wanna be going to the Uncle Josh Part do ya?' said the driver.

'Well, if that's where Temple Avenue is, I guess you're correct,' said Grandad with a bit of chuckle.

Lydia sat in between Dad and Grandad in the taxi, quietly giggling to herself. 'Excuse me, may I ask you a question?' she asked the driver.

'Of course, fire away,' he replied.

'Can you please explain to me what an Uncle Josh part is? I'm a little bit confused,' she said with a smile, trying not to offend him.

'An Uncle Josh part? It's cockney for a posh part,' he replied.
'A posh part? What do you mean?'
'Temple Avenue is where all of them barristers, solicitors, and judges are. It's a very posh place in London, indeed, it is.'
'Why didn't you say that in the first place?' Lydia laughed. 'What is your name? And how long have you been driving taxis?'
'Lydia, will you stop asking the gentleman so many questions,' said Dad, quietly.
'Sorry, Dad, I'm just intrigued, that's all.'
'I understand that Lydia, but you are coming across a little bit nosy. He may not want to tell you all of his business.'
'Your father's right. Maybe he does not want to answer your questions,' said Grandad while tapping his hand gently on her cheek.

The taxi driver looked in his rear-view mirror and saw that Lydia's father and grandfather were talking to one another, while Lydia was looking slightly glum.

'It's all right, guvna, I don't mind answering her questions,' he said. I've been a London taxi driver for the best part of thirty years. I know these streets like the back of 'me hand I do, and if you don't already know, my name is Arthur and it's pleasure meeting you all.'

'Thank you very much, Arthur, for answering my questions,' Lydia replied.

'No worries.'

She told Arthur that she had never been to London before and was excited to visit the city, even after the long, tedious train journey.

'I'll tell you what, Lydia, meaning as you haven't been to ol' Smoke before I'll take you on a little tour of London on your way to Rubbelswick's. I'll take you past Buckingham Palace—she's a real beauty—and if the flag is flying, it means Queen Elizabeth is at home,' said Arthur.

'I'd like that enormously, Arthur,' thank you.' She then turned to Grandad. 'What's the big smoke?' she asked quietly, not wishing to ask Arthur too many questions.

'It means London.'

'Do we have time for Arthur to take us past Buckingham Palace?'

'Yes, we have time,' Dad smiled.

Lydia was thrilled. 'We would like that very much, Arthur, and if you like Buckingham Palace, then you'd love Gwendonia Castle. She is enormous and the grandest castle that ever stood.'

'She sounds a lovely castle, Lydia, but have you seen Windsor Castle? Another beauty so she is,' said Arthur. 'But when I next visit Wales, I'll be sure to come by and have a look at the old girl.'

Lydia immediately thought of the stranger in the woods, who had also referred to the castle as an 'old girl'.

As Arthur drove them around the sights of London, Lydia stared at the city in amazement. 'Look, Dad, there's Big Ben! There's Tower Bridge! And the Tower of London!'

As they passed Buckingham Palace, Arthur said,' 'Sorry, but I'm afraid the Queen ain't home today—see? There's no flag flying. Never mind, maybe next time, eh?'

'That's OK, Arthur,' said Lydia. 'I'm so pleased that you have taken me around London— it was so very kind of you.'

'You're very welcome, Lydia,' said Arthur, with an enormous grin on his face.

Arthur drove into Temple Avenue, and the taxi slowly pulled up outside Rubbelswick Chambers. 'We're here,' said Arthur. Lydia looked out of the back cab window, tilting her head back to see the full scale of the building. It was an old, imposing looking structure, with captivating marble sculptures carved into its façade.

Above the front double doors, a large, elaborate sign with gold lettering read:

RUBBELSWICK CHAMBERS Est 1776

Lydia stepped out of the taxi and noticed several figures with long, flowing black gowns, wearing grey wigs and holding bundles of court documents. They were barristers, coming and going out of the various law chambers situated all the way along the avenue.

'Told ya it's posh, didn't I?' said Arthur, grinning as he stuck his head out of the cab window.

'They all look so *regal*, don't they, Arthur? Especially with the wigs and the cloaks. I've never seen a barrister before, except on TV. There aren't any where I live. They must all live in London,' said Lydia jokingly.

'It's time to say goodbye to Arthur,' said Lydia's father.

'Goodbye, Arthur,' said Lydia, who felt that, even thought she had only just met him, she had known Arthur from some time before. It was a bizarre feeling indeed.

'Take care of yourself, Lydia, and say hello to Lady Ronan for me.'

Lydia was shocked. 'How did you know Lady Ronan?'

'What do you mean *knew*?' replied Arthur, in a concerned tone.

'I'm so sorry, Arthur, but Lady Ronan passed away. How did you know her?'

'I knew Lady Ronan for many years. I would collect her from Paddington train station and take her to meetings at Rubbelswick Chambers. She would often speak of her home. When you mentioned the castle, I knew instantly that you were talking about Lady Ronan's Gwendonia,' replied Arthur.

Lydia noticed that he was shocked by the news of her passing and did not want to ask any more questions, for fear of further upsetting him.

'Come,' Lydia,' said Dad, who pacing outside the entrance to the chambers, 'we're going to be late for our appointment. Thank you, Arthur, for the tour of London, and it was also a pleasure meeting you!'

'Goodbye, Lydia! Just remember—there will always be people around who will keep you safe and protected. Always remember what I have told you: be brave; you are destined for great things,' said Arthur.

Before Lydia could reply, Arthur drove off, waving to her from his window, and she watched until the taxi had disappeared from view.

'Lydia, hurry,' called Dad, as he pushed the door open to enter the chambers. 'We only have five minutes until we meet with Mr Rubbelswick!

They entered the building and made their way to a woman sitting at the front desk. 'Can I help you, sir?' she asked.

'Yes, we have an appointment with Mr Rubbelswick at 12.30pm,' said Lydia's father.

'It's Mr Daniel Rose.'

'Do please take a seat, Mr Rose. Is there anything I can get for you? Anything at all?' asked the woman.

'No, thank you,' replied Lydia's father.

'I don't know what all this fuss is about. Why are we here? Surely Rubbelswick could have discussed whatever is going on with me over the telephone,' said Dad.

'All will be revealed shortly. I'm sure we won't be taking up too much of his time; he's probably a very busy man. We'll be in and out in minutes, I'm sure. I have the key to the garden entrance of Gwendonia . Perhaps that's what he wants?' said Grandad.

Lydia was getting the impression that Grandad felt uncomfortable being in the Chambers, as though he wasn't good enough or educated enough to converse with the likes of Rubbelswick. Lydia felt the need to reassure Grandad and told him he looked like a gentleman in his smart suit and trench coat.

'I'm a gardener, Lydia. I'm not used to frequenting such places,' he smiled nervously.

Lydia held his hand and squeezed it gently, 'You're the best gentleman there is Grandad; there is no one like you.'

'Thank you very much, my sweet girl.'

Lydia's father was pacing up and down the foyer. 'I wish he'd hurry up and call us in; we don't want to miss our train home, we might . . . you know, get stuck in the London traffic.'

Lydia's grandfather was sitting silently, looking around at the opulence of the reception area. 'I'm sure we'll be called in shortly.'

The receptionist stood up from behind her desk. 'Mr Rubbelswick will see you now. Please follow me.'

'Thank goodness,' said Lydia's father.

As they walked down a long corridor, they could see lots of people in offices, busily at work.

Lydia, Dad, and Grandad soon found themselves standing outside Mr Rubbelswick's office. The receptionist led them in.

'Miss Lydia Rose, Mr Daniel Rose, and Mr John Rose, sir,' she announced, and left, closing the door gently behind her.

'Ah! Come, come, please do sit down! Is there anything I can get you? Maybe a refreshment? Tea? Coffee? Some juice, perhaps?' asked Rubbelswick.

'No, thank you,' they all replied.

Mr Rubbelswick was not what they had expected at all, and their anxieties melted away as he talked. He came across as rather a friendly and approachable middle-aged man.

Lydia couldn't take her eyes off Mr Rubbelswick. He was a short, stout, balding man with round, rosy cheeks. He had a friendly face, with a pair of round, wire glasses perched on the tip of his nose. *I hope he doesn't sneeze, as they would surely end up on his desk*, thought Lydia. Mr Rubbelswick was wearing a dark suit and a white shirt—clearly too small— through which his belly bulged, placing enormous pressure on his shirt buttons. Lydia was confident that if he moved too quickly, his buttons would shoot out like darts towards her. His tie, knotted around his chubby, round neck, looked as if it might choke him.

'I suppose you're all wondering why I have requested to see you?' said Rubbelswick.

'Yes, though I'm sure we could have had discussed whatever it is over the telephone instead of coming all this way to see you,' said Lydia's father.

'Not exactly, Mr Rose. I don't feel that what I have to say to you all could have been communicated over the telephone.'

Lydia looked at Dad and Grandad while chewing the inside of her cheek nervously, and thinking, *What if Rubbelswick knows that I trespassed onto Gwendonia? Is he going to tell my father, and will he get fined?* Tormented, she slipped her hand into her coat pocket and held the Lamanya Stone tightly in her hand. She couldn't wait for Rubbelswick to get on with why they were required to attend his office.

'I'm very aware that you all knew the Late Lady Ronan and, when she would visit the chambers, she would often talk about you all—and especially you Miss Lydia! Yes, she was extremely fond of you. I, for one, will miss her immensely,' said Rubbelswick, in a low voice.

40

'We are all in complete shock. I worked for Lady Ronan for more than forty years, and I will miss her tremendously. And not being able to work at Gwendonia again . . . well, that will be hard for me,' said Grandad.

'We all miss her. I knew her all my life,' said Dad.

'Then I'd best get on with it!' Rubbelswick proceeded to rummage through a large pile of legal papers on his desk; some had several coffee ring stains stamped on them from his coffee cup. 'Now, where did I put them?' he muttered aloud, 'Blast, blast, blast . . . Aha! Here there they are, right, let's get to it.'

The Roses sat around the table on the edges of their seats, waiting for Mr Rubbleswick to speak.

'Lady Ronan made a will and has left Gwendonia castle to Lydia. Splendid, wouldn't you say?'

'What do you mean?' said Dad, feeling somewhat overwhelmed.

'What I just said, Mr Rose! Lydia is the owner of Gwendonia,' he replied.

'But she is only 12 years old!' he gasped, bemused by the news.

Lydia and Grandad sat in shock, looking at each other in amazement. *I was worrying for nothing! Rubbelswick didn't know that I had trespassed onto Gwendonia, and now I own it!* Lydia thought.

'Let me finish, Mr Rose, there is more to get through, a whole lot more. Lydia owns the castle but you and your wife, as her parents, will be custodians until her 25th birthday.'

'Then there is a trust fund for Ellis Rose, your son—a very nice trust fund indeed, left for him by the late Lady Ronan.'

'May I ask a question?' asked Lydia.

'Ask away,' replied Rubbelswick.

'Didn't Lady Ronan have any family or relatives to leave all her things to?

'No, I'm afraid she didn't. Her will had been written for many years, and she was sure who she would leave everything to,' he replied.

Rubbelswick continued to read through the will of the late Lady Ronan and informed Lydia, Dad, and Grandad that all her jewellery, furniture, and businesses would be shared equally between Lydia, Mr Daniel Rose, and Mr John Rose.

'You have been left a vast fortune, a substantial amount,' Rubbelswick told them. 'And you, dear Lydia, must have been an exceptional girl to be the object of such generosity, Lady Ronan had received several offers to sell the castle, but she declined each one. She once told me, "Rubbelswick, I can understand why so many people wish to buy the castle, but I will never sell".'

'I don't know what to say, I truly can't believe that we have Gwendonia. We get to live there? I will never sell Gwendonia either, Mr Rubbelswick. Even when I get old.'

'I can't quite believe it,' said Grandad, still looking shocked.

'Grandad, I told you there was no need to worry, didn't I? We are no different to anyone else and now we can help other people. Lady Ronan told me that.'

'What do you mean?' asked Grandad inquisitively.

'Lady Ronan told me you should always help someone less fortunate than yourself. Not just by giving them money, but also by giving them your time.'

'You are far too grown-up,' Lydia. You are destined for great things,' I'm sure,' Grandad smiled.

For a moment Lydia sat thinking to herself: *Why is everyone telling me that I'm destined for great things? I'm only 12 years old and live in a quiet place where nothing much happens.*

'Rest assured, Mr Rubbelswick, we will take great care of Gwendonia, just as lady Ronan did,' said Dad.

'How did you know Lady Ronan, Mr Rubbelswick?' asked Lydia.

'Don't you know Lydia? Lady Ronan's ancestors founded and set up these law chambers in 1776. Lady Ronan owned these chambers, and since deciding to sell half of the business to me five years ago, I had worked closely with her. Now, your family are joint owners of these chambers, and I look forward to doing business with you in the future.

'I can appreciate the enormity of what I have told you, and our meeting has taken longer than expected. There has been a lot to discuss,' he said with a chuckle, 'and I'm afraid the time has ticked on. You might not be on time to catch your train home.

Let me make a hotel reservation for you all to stay overnight in London. What do you say, Mr Rose?' Rubbelswick beamed.

'I suppose you're right, it's likely that we will miss our train, so yes, thank you. We'll take you up on your offer,' replied Lydia's father. 'We'll stay here in London overnight.'

'Splendid, splendid! I'll book you into the Ritz Hotel; a fine hotel. I'm sure you'll find it quite satisfactory. Lady Ronan always stayed there when she would visit London.

'And thank you all for meeting with me! As you can appreciate, this conversation needed to be had face to face and couldn't have been done over the telephone.'

'I agree that there was far too much to discuss. Even though it's been a long day,' said Lydia's father, laughing. 'I can't quite believe what's happened, Mr Rubbelswick. It's surreal. Never in our wildest dreams would we have expected such an outcome. I really can't comprehend it at all.'

'Yes, yes, I'm sure! A life-changing day for you all,' said Rubbelswick. 'If you make your way back down to the foyer, my assistant will call a cab to take you to the Ritz. Have a lovely evening! I'll be in touch soon, Mr Rose.'

'Thank you, Mr Rubbelswick, for your time,' said Lydia's father and grandfather.

''Bye, Mr Rubbelswick,' said Lydia.

''Bye to you too, Lydia, and look after Gwendonia. I hear she's an enchanted castle.' Mr Rubbelswick was sounding very cheerful indeed.

Lydia giggled. 'It is wonderful, but I wouldn't describe it as enchanted.'

'Really? It is not what I've been told.' He raised an eyebrow.

'I'll be sure to let you know if I bump into any goblins, fairies or evil creatures,' she replied.

'You never know, stranger things have happened,' he said, and winked. Lydia recollected the unusual event that had taken place at the castle: perhaps the Asiras had moved after all.

'I have never seen anything unusual or out of the ordinary. But I'm sure Gwendonia holds many secrets,' said Grandad.

'You obviously didn't look hard enough, Mr Rose,'' said Rubbelswick, chuckling.

The Roses made their way to the foyer and out to where the cab, which was waiting to take them to the hotel. Lydia was eager to see who the taxi driver would be, hoping it would be Arthur. She was soon disappointed.

'Did you hope that Arthur would be here, Lydia?' asked Grandad.

'Yes— it would have been great to tell him the news of the castle. I'm sure he would have been pleased.'

'You never know, you might bump into him some day.'

Soon, they were at the Ritz, and it was just as splendid as Mr Rubbelswick had described. They were shown to their hotel suite, which was very lavish, and Lydia couldn't contain her excitement.

'Mum, Gran, and even Ellis would love it here,' she enthused.

Lydia's father laughed. 'I'm sure they would! I'll be telephoning home shortly to let them know that we'll be staying overnight in London.'

'I'm starving. I'm going to eat everything on the menu!' Lydia chuckled.

'Yes, I could do with something to eat. We haven't eaten since the train,' said Grandad.

Having made their way to the hotel restaurant, they were shown to their table. 'So, this is where Lady Ronan would have come for dinner?' commented Lydia.

'Most likely,' replied Dad.

'Don't you think it's lovely?' Lydia kept saying, as she gazed around the restaurant.

'It is spectacular. I have never been in a restaurant or hotel as posh as this, Lydia, never in my life,' replied Grandad.

'But Grandad, you are now, and you can order anything you like on the menu.'

'You know, I will have a look to see what I can order.'

Lydia's grandfather stuck his head into the menu and began moaning about the prices. 'Have you noticed how much a glass of wine is? And lobster? You could buy four lobsters where we live for the price of one lobster here!'

Lydia found Grandad's comments amusing and began chuckling.

'Go on, Lydia, you can pick anything you like on the menu,' said Dad.

'Can I really? It's very expensive.'

'Choose what you would like,' replied Dad.

'In that case, please may I have a roast dinner with mint sauce and lots of gravy, followed by a knickerbocker glory, with lashings of fresh cream, strawberry sauce, and sprinkles, please.'

'Then that's what you'll have,' said Dad. 'I think we'll all have the same.'

I'm not ordering the lobster, that's for sure,' said Grandad, still annoyed over the menu prices.

Lydia's father and grandfather were talking together while Lydia put her hand into her dress pocket and took out the Lamanya Stone. She held it in her hand, staring at it, and thinking about Lady Ronan. She thanked her for everything she had done for her and her family.

'What's that you are looking at?' Dad and grandfather asked inquisitively.

'It's the Lamanya Stone. Lady Ronan gave it to me—the afternoon tea day,' said Lydia quietly. 'She said it would protect me from evil.'

'Whatever do you mean?' asked Grandad.

'Lady Ronan told me to always keep it safe, as it will protect me from all that's evil,' she explained.

'Right,' he responded, 'if that's what it is, that's great. I thought it was more of a decorative piece—not some talisman to ward off evil! Keep it safe,' said Grandad.

Lydia placed the Lamanya Stone on the table next to her. She occasionally glanced at it while eating her dinner. The restaurant was full of diners, and people coming and going. As Lydia was tucking into her dessert, she gasped as she noticed that the angels inside the stone were moving, with terror etched on their faces.

'What's wrong?' asked Dad.

'N-n-nothing, just that the ice cream is cold, that's all! I've got brain freeze.' She picked up the stone and quickly put it back into her pocket. She looked around the restaurant, observing the different faces, trying to figure out the cause of the angels' terrified expressions.

45

It continued to play on Lydia's mind, so she asked Dad and grandfather if could she return to the hotel room. 'Yes, I think we'll call it a night. It's been a very long day, and we need to get to Paddington early to catch our train home,' said Lydia's father. Back in the confines of their hotel suite, Lydia felt safe.

'Can you imagine their faces, Grandad, when we tell Gran, Mum, and Ellis, what's happened to us? They will never believe it.'

'I'm sure they'll be shocked, just as we were,' replied Grandad.

When Lydia went to her bedroom, she was reluctant to take the stone out of her pocket for fear that the angels would still have the same terrifying look on their faces as they'd had in the restaurant. However, she took the stone from her pocket and to her relief, their faces looked serene and peaceful and she felt calmer.

It must have been someone in the restaurant that caused the stone to change, she thought. But who would want to harm her? The responsibility of the stone and the danger it seemed to detect made her feel anxious. She even considered hiding the stone in her bedside draw, when she returned home, but she soon dismissed the thought. *I promised Lady Ronan that I would always keep it by my side, and that's what I'm going to do.*

It was morning; and following breakfast Roses returned to Paddington to catch their train back to Wales. 'Look what has happened to us in 24 hours. It is genuinely remarkable,' said Lydia's father.

'It's unbelievable,' Grandad and Lydia replied.

'Soon, we will all be living in Gwendonia Castle. How do you feel about that Lydia? Are you excited'? Dad asked.

'Excited, happy, and a little sad that Lady Ronan will no longer be there.'

'Lady Ronan will always be with you, as long as you keep her memory in your heart,' said Grandad.

'I know.'

Finally, they were on their way home to Roselee House. In a short while, the Rose family would be moving into majestic Gwendonia Castle. Only then would they know for sure if the castle would reveal its secrets.

Chapter 5

The Majestic Gwendonia

Roselee House was full of joy following the events of London, as the Rose family prepared to move into Gwendonia Castle. It was a surreal time, and the family still couldn't quite believe what the past few days had brought them.

Three days later, the family left Roselee House. There were people everywhere packing, carrying, and moving things.

'Don't forget to take all the valuables, and photos,' shouted Gran.

'I've already packed them,' replied Mum.

Ellis was busy cleaning the yard and tending to his pet goose. 'I'm taking Eggbert with us. He's not staying here,' Ellis told his father.

'You'll need to make sure the pen is locked, as we don't want another performance do we Ellis?' his father laughed. 'If he escapes at the castle, you'll never find him again, that's for certain.'

'I know Dad,' said Ellis, huffing.

'Oh my, I'd forgotten how beautiful and huge Gwendonia is! I haven't been here for ages,' said Lydia's mother, when they finally arrived.

'Me neither! She looks big when you see her from Roselee House, but when you're up close to her, she is truly colossal,' said Gran.

Lydia's father and grandfather were used to the enormity of Gwendonia and neither of them appeared to be fazed by its size.

Lydia was feeling overwhelmed. As she gazed at the castle she felt upset, knowing that Lady Ronan wouldn't be inside. However, the family would take care of the 'old girl' now.

Once inside the castle, Ellis was shouting, 'I can't believe it we live here!' He ran off through the passages, looking for his bedroom.

'Even though there are at least 40 bedrooms in this castle, not including Lady Ronan's, you're next to me,' said Lydia.

'Just like being at Roselee, we're all close by,' said Ellis excitedly. 'I'm not sleeping in Lady Ronan's bedroom though—it'd give me the creeps. I bet it's massive with all girly things.'

'No one is having her room, Ellis. It'll always be Lady Ronan's room, and it'll be just as she left it,' said Lydia.

'Why was her bedroom in the round tower, when it's all the way over the other side of the castle? asked Ellis.

'I don't really know, but she had a lovely view of St Cein's church,' replied Lydia.

'I for one won't be going in there because of ghosts, Lyd. Ghosts—she'll haunt the castle in the night, and anyone who snoops through her belongings,' he said in a scary voice, trying to frighten her.

'She never harmed me when she was alive, and I'm sure she wouldn't harm me now that she's dead. She was lovely Ellis. You never knew her like I did,' Lydia explained.

'No, I know, I'm only teasing you. She must have really liked you to leave her castle to you,' said Ellis,' seeming sincere. 'Just think! We could hide in this castle and neither Mum nor Dad would never find us! Isn't that brilliant? We'll have to explore the whole of this place—it's enormous!'

'Ellis! Lydia!' called out Gran. 'Help! I don't know my way around here. I go through one door and end up somewhere completely different,' she laughed.

'You'll be fine, Gran! You'll find your way around, you'll get used to it, in about two years!' Ellis said, laughing.

'Don't you be so daft, Ellis. I'll be OK in a week or two! I just need to get my bearings, that's all. You could fit Roselee House and its gardens in this place at least 50 times!' she said.

'Where do you need to go Gran?' asked Lydia.

'I was hoping to go outside and have a look around, that's all: see the garden and all the lovely flowers.'

Lydia walked her gran through the castle and led her out to the castle grounds.

'I know your grandfather is out here somewhere,' said Gran, laughing. 'John! John! Where are you?' she called.

Lydia shook her head laughing at her grandmother's high-pitched voice calling out for Grandad. Lydia left Gran in the gardens and quickly returned to her bedroom. Ellis had started lugging boxes of their belongings into both of their bedrooms. Lydia's and Ellis's rooms were in the castle turrets, and both had impressive views overlooking the sea and mountains. They were large rooms, with huge four-poster beds. As Lydia gazed through the bedroom window, she could hear a loud, clanking noise coming from Ellis's bedroom.

'Lydia, hurry! Come and look at my bedroom! Quick, come and look!'

Lydia rushed into her brother's bedroom. 'What's wrong? Why are you shouting?' she asked.

'Nothing is wrong! Look, I've got two armoured knights in my room! no girly things anywhere. Look, aren't they brilliant?' he said. The suits of armour, facing towards Ellis's bed, looked just like real knights in their shining armour, and holding swords in their gloved hands. 'They'll keep me safe from the castle ghosts,' Ellis laughed.

'Will you stop with the ghost thing? It's getting boring now,' Lydia scoffed.

'You know the noise you heard? The clanking sounds?

'Yes.'

'It was me, trying to move these heavy things. I won't be able to go to sleep with them looking and glaring at me, no way,' he said in a panicked tone.

'What's wrong? Afraid of ghosts, are we?'

'No! They're shiny, that's all, and they'll dazzle my eyes. I won't be able to get any sleep, you know what I mean,' he mumbled.

'Yeah right,' Lydia laughed. 'Just admit that you're scared. Shall I get Dad to help move them? Do you think they might come alive and attack you in the dead of night with their swords?' she said teasingly.

'I'm not scared, I just want to move them to another part of my room, that's all,' he replied. 'They are cool though! I'm going to name them Lancelot and—'

'—Don't tell me, Arthur?'

'Yeah! How did you guess that?'.

'I don't know really, it just popped into my head. It must be the ghosts letting me know what you're thinking,' she replied

'Really?' Ellis said in a shocked tone.

'No Ellis, Arthur and the Knights of the Round Table? You've obviously read the book,' she reminded him.

'Oh yeah, I forgot about that.'

'I'm starving! Come on, let's try to find another way to the kitchen,' said Lydia. 'I wonder if Mum and Gran have found the kitchen yet?' she said. They laughed and ran down one of the long passages leading to one of the many back staircases.

'Are you sure you know where you're going?' asked Ellis, who was out of breath from running.

'No, just follow me, we'll soon find out,' said Lydia.

They finally came to the bottom of a long staircase and found themselves standing outside a large wooden door.

'Open it Lyd,' said Ellis.

'I'm trying! What do you think I'm doing?' she snapped, pushing as hard as she could. 'Help me, don't just stand there! You push too.'

They both began pushing the door as hard as they could.

'It's stuck, it's not budging,' said Ellis, frustrated. With that, the door burst open, and both fell onto the kitchen floor and began laughing hysterically.

'Good gracious, what on earth are you two doing?' said Gran, who was startled by their entrance.

'We were trying to find the kitchen by going a different way, Gran,' they responded.

'You found it then, and made quite an entrance, that's for sure!' she said, smiling while stirring the vegetables cooking on the large Aga stove.

'We're having a roast dinner, with all the trimmings,' said their grandmother.

'Gran, don't give me any broccoli, otherwise I'll be playing music all night,' said Ellis, while laughing.

'Don't be so disgusting, your bedroom is next to mine and it will seep like poison under my bedroom door and I'll be unconscious from the smell,' said Lydia. Both Lydia and Ellis were aching with laughter.

'You pair better stop that talk at once, and stop messing about! Make yourselves useful and lay the dinner table,' said Gran. Ellis and Lydia pinched a roast potato each and began to lay the table while still giggling.

'What's so amusing? What are you two laughing about?' asked Mum.

'Nothing really Mum, only that Ellis was talking about farting,' Lydia replied, giggling.

'Oh Ellis! Please, that's disgusting, enough of that talk.'

Lydia and Ellis smirked at each other as they continued to lay the table in the dining room. There were three dining rooms in the castle, but they had decided on the least formal of the three.

'Ah, there you all are,' said Dad. 'It's good to see that you're both helping your mother. Have you managed to sort out your bedrooms?'

'Yes, we have Dad,' replied Lydia. 'Ellis and I both have big, fairy-tale turret bedrooms overlooking the sea,' Lydia smiled.

'I thought all our bedrooms would be by each other, in case either of you needed us in the night. I don't want you to have bedrooms on the other side of the castle,' said their father.

'We love our bedrooms, they're perfect ' replied Lydia and Ellis.

'Have you two seen Lady Ronan's cats, by any chance?' asked their father.

'Cats? What cats?' replied Lydia.

'Black cats: two of them. They are always wandering around the battlements and outside Lady Ronan's bedroom. They tend to roam all around the castle. You must have noticed them, surely?'

'No, we haven't Dad,' they responded. Lydia thought it odd that she had never seen them, even though she has been visiting the castle for years.

'Are they friendly, Dad?' asked Ellis.

'Yes, they're friendly. They must be years old. Well, if you see them, let me know, as they'll need to be fed.'

'I'll keep a look-out, Dad, but I'm not going to look for them anywhere near Lady Ronan's room.'

'Why ever not?' asked his father, puzzled.

'Here we go again! Ghosts. Ellis thinks Lady Ronan's room is creepy, and it's all the way over in the round tower and he's afraid that she'll haunt him,' said Lydia.

'Ellis, don't be silly,' said Dad.

'I just don't like the round tower, that's all, it's a bit strange. There is no one over that part of the castle; its eerie,' replied Ellis.

'There wouldn't be anyone over there, would there? It's only us living here for the time being. It's only until all of the staff return to work here, as we can't run this place on our own,' their father told them.

'I'm so glad that Cook and all the other staff will be coming back to work at Gwendonia; it'll be just like before, well, almost,' enthused Lydia.

'Yes, it will certainly liven up the place,' said Dad, laughing.

'What's all this laughing?' asked Grandad.

'Grandad, isn't it great? All the staff are coming back to the castle,' said Lydia.

'I thought you might like it that Cook and the others will be returning,' he said, smiling.

Suddenly, their conversation was interrupted when a gentle voice called out. 'Hello, can I come in?' It was Father David, from St Cein's Church.

'Come in, Father David, and make yourself at home,' said Mum.

Gran had invited Father David to join them for dinner. As they all sat around the dining table, eating and engaging in lively chatter,' Lydia looked at each person and realised how lucky she was to be with her family and Father David, who was a lovely, mellow gentleman. He had been the vicar of St Cein's for more than 50 years and was also a close and dear friend to the late Lady Ronan.

'I think you will all love living here, I know Lady Ronan wouldn't have lived anywhere else,' said Father David, smiling.

'Yes, I'm sure we will, Father David,' replied Dad.

Lydia was now living in Gwendonia, her favourite place in the world. Dinner had finished, and both Lydia and Ellis said goodnight to their family and Father David. It was time for them to go to bed: after all, it had been a long and exciting day.

'I'll race you upstairs and we'll go the long way round, past those creepy things, you know, those marble statues, and then up the great staircase,' said Ellis.

'You'll get lost, I bet,' said Lydia, chuckling.

'No I won't,' he replied, 'On the count of three, 1, 2, 3 . . . go!' said Ellis.

They both began running at speed along the passageways, laughing while grabbing each other to prevent the other from getting ahead.

'I'm winning! I'm winning!' yelled Ellis.

'Only just!' Lydia shouted out, as she began to catch him up.

They got lost several times trying to find their way to the grand staircase.

'Here we are, found it,' said Lydia. They had stopped running and paused to look at the marble statues.

'Look at those things—they're so life-like,' said Ellis, while poking at their faces with his finger and shuddering. 'Why would you want something that looked so human? Creepy things,' he said as he began walking up the staircase.

'I think they are quite beautiful,' said Lydia, stroking the face on the female statue while gazing into her eyes. In her peripheral vision she thought she saw the head of the male statue turn around and look at her. She froze, too afraid to move. 'Ellis! Ellis! Ellis!' she screamed.

Ellis was at the top of the staircase. 'What's wrong? Why are you screaming?'

'Did you see? Did you see?' she said, whilst hyperventilating.

'See what?'

'It moved! It really moved! It was looking at me,' said Lydia, panicking.

'What moved? And by the way, Lyd, you really are a good actress. You should think of it as a possible career choice,' he said, laughing.

'Wh . . .wh . . .what are you talking about? It really moved, Ellis, I'm telling you! The head of the male statue moved. I'm not lying to you,' she stuttered.

'Oh, I see what you're doing, you're trying to frighten me before I go to bed with my knights of armour.'

53

'No, I'm really not, I know what I saw . . . like when I saw the cherubs, the Asiras! The cherubs are called Asiras and they moved when I had afternoon tea with Lady Ronan,' she said sternly.

'You are not making any sense,' said Ellis.

'Do you see these?' she pointed to the cherubs, 'they're everywhere, they're on the balustrade! In the cornice! They are all around the castle, Ellis. If you look for them, you'll see them. Well, that's what Cook said.'

Ellis was a little concerned, as he had never before seen Lydia in such a panicked state.

'OK,' OK. I believe you,' said Ellis.

'No, you don't, you are just saying that to make me feel better,' Lydia sighed.

'Come on, I'll walk you up to your bedroom. You're probably tired, that's all,' he reassured her.

'What if this castle really is enchanted, Ellis?'

'What do you mean? If it comes alive?'

'Yes, that's exactly what I mean.'

'Ah, don't say that! If it's enchanted, the knights will come alive, and they have swords. I'll be sleeping with my light on tonight, that's for sure,' he said, panicking.

'There is something strange happening, Ellis, and I don't quite know what it is,' she said calmly.

'Everything will be normal in the morning, you'll see. Now get some sleep and you'll be fine,' he said reassuringly.

As they reached their bedrooms, Ellis told Lydia, 'If you need me, knock on my door, OK?'

'Thanks, Ellis. I'll see you in the morning.' They went into their bedrooms, and soon fell into a deep sleep.

The sound of scratching coming from outside her bedroom door woke Lydia in the early hours. She quickly sat up in bed, turned on her bed-side lamp, and walked slowly towards her door, her heart pounding out of her chest. She could still hear noises outside. Frightened, she stood there silently, shaking all over and her hands trembling with fear.

What if the marble figures had come alive? And they were standing outside her door? She remained still for a few more minutes, until finally she found the courage to slowly open the door. She couldn't believe what she was seeing. Two black cats were sitting on the floor. *They must be Lady Ronan's cats*, Lydia thought. One of them was carrying something small in its mouth, which it dropped at her feet.

As Lydia knelt down to study what looked like a small ball of fur, the two cats disappeared down the passageway. The ball of fur began squeaking. It was a tiny fox cub, the smallest cub she'd ever seen.

'Aww, aren't you the cutest thing?' She picked up the fox cub, cuddled it and took it into her bedroom, where she noticed a small note attached to its collar. *What on earth is going on?* she thought. *Why did a cat come to my door at 2am with a fox cub in its mouth? Very odd indeed.* The cub snuggled up on Lydia's bed and fell fast asleep. She opened the note and began to read.

 '*The one called Skrinkle they will send, who will protect and guide you to the end.*'

Lydia thought then that Ellis had played a joke on her, but she knew her brother wouldn't have written a rhyme, or have found a fox cub. Lydia's thoughts quickly returned to the fox cub: she needed to hide it. She opened the lid on the ottoman at the bottom of her bed and placed it inside, before gently closing the lid. Satisfied that it was safe, she got back into bed and fell into a deep sleep.

It was morning. 'Breakfast is ready!' called Dad.

Lydia was sitting on the edge of her bed, with thoughts of the previous night going around her head. 'Oh, the fox cub!' Without any hesitation, she opened the lid of the ottoman and saw the fox cub sitting up with what appeared to be a little grin on its face, its big, watery, green eyes looking directly at her. 'Please don't make any noise, I'll go and get some food for you,' she whispered.

'Lydia! Are you coming for breakfast?' called Ellis from outside her bedroom door.

'Yes, I'm coming.'

As they walked down the passage, Ellis still appeared concerned about his sister's erratic behaviour from the previous night.

'Are you OK, really?

'Yes, I'm fine! I was convinced I saw that statue move though, Ellis.' Lydia wanted to tell him about the cats, the fox and the note, but for some reason she couldn't and kept it to herself.

'Well, the knights didn't come alive, so this castle can't be enchanted,' he chuckled. 'Are you sure you're OK?' asked Ellis again, still concerned.

'Yes, thanks for asking but I'm OK, really. Let's go and get some breakfast and then we'll go and explore the castle, what do you say?' she said.

'Sounds great, but don't run off Lyd, there are so many rooms and passages I know that I'd get lost.'

'We'll stay together, I promise,' she reassured him.

At breakfast, Ellis noticed Lydia smuggle fruit and eggs into a napkin and put them into her pocket.

'I'll be just a minute, wait for me here Ellis,' Lydia asked.

'OK,' he mumbled, with his mouth full.

Lydia ran up the back stairs, as she didn't want to pass the statues by the grand staircase for fear she would see them move again. She ran into her bedroom, opened the ottoman and took out the fox cub, placing him on the floor.

She took the glass of water from her bedside cabinet. The fox munched his way through the food on the napkin, and while Lydia held the glass, he began lapping water from it with his little tongue.

'You are the cutest cub I have ever seen. Is your name Skrinkle?' she asked. The cub looked up at her. Lydia wondered where the fox cub had come from. It climbed onto her lap and snuggled into her. 'I'll keep you here until you're a little bigger. You'll be safe here. I'll be back soon, Skrinkle, I must go, otherwise my brother will come looking for me. Do you understand? Just please stay quiet, I'll be back soon, I promise.'

'Lydia? Where are you?' shouted Ellis.

'I'm coming Ellis!' she shouted, and ran out of her bedroom, closing her door tightly behind her.

How could she tell her family about the cats bringing the fox cub to her bedroom door at 2am? How could she explain the turning head of the marble statue?

Lydia had an overwhelming feeling that she needed to visit the round tower. However, she had no choice but to wait until everyone had retired to bed and the castle was locked. She decided that it would be that night. She would secretly make her way to the round tower.

Chapter 6

Secrets Of The Round Tower

Everyone had finally gone to bed. There was total silence; not a sound could be heard in the castle. It was Lydia's chance to go to the round tower and visit Lady Ronan's bedroom without anyone following her. It was 1am when Lydia's curiosity finally took hold of her. She checked the corridor outside her bedroom: there wasn't a soul to be found. She put on her dressing gown, tied a knot in her belt and put on her slippers.

Skrinkle was fast asleep at the bottom of her bed. She opened her bedroom door quietly and closed it gently behind her. *I can't put on the lights; I'll need to use my torch to see my way*, she thought.

Outside her bedroom door she switched on her torch; its glow lit up the long dark passage. She began walking slowly, with the torchlight making gigantic shadows on the walls. For a split second, Lydia thought about abandoning her plans and returning to the comfort of her bedroom, but she continued, through numerous long, dark passages and several doors, to the round tower. It was pitch-black, apart from the light of her torch.

I know Lady Ronan is with me; I just know it, she thought to herself, as she continued to walk.

Finally, she reached the doorway that led to the round tower.

Anxious, she stood outside the door to compose herself for several seconds, her heart pounding fast. She took several deep breaths before slowly opening the door and walked down the long corridor leading to Lady Ronan's bedroom. The torch shone all around and up towards the ceiling, behind her, towards the floor, and then straight ahead. Lydia almost dropped her torch when something startled her. In the distance were four small, still lights. Slowly, she moved towards them, trying to make out what they were.

'Ah, it's you!' she said, feeling relieved. The two black cats approached her, their eyes reflecting in the torchlight.

'What are you doing all the way over here? You miss her, don't you?' said Lydia, stroking both their heads. It was upsetting seeing them sitting there, as though they were waiting for her. They were friendly cats, and they began to curl affectionately around her feet. Stroking them with one hand, Lydia opened Lady Ronan's bedroom door with the other.

The cats quickly jumped up onto the bed and sat almost statue-like. Lydia felt confident that her parents and grandparents wouldn't be able to see any lights from the other side of the castle and turned on the bedside lamp. The bedroom was huge, with a large, four-poster bed, carved bedside cabinets, a writing desk, a dressing table, and a large, white marble fireplace. Huge family portraits and captivating tapestries adorned the walls. Lydia wandered around Lady Ronan's elegant bedroom, taking in the opulence. On one of the bedroom walls she noticed the largest, most intricate and beguiling wood carving that she had ever seen. It was enormous: it stretched from the floor to the ceiling. It was like a scene from a fairy tale. There were fairies, elves, dragons, castles, and the detail was exquisite.

She began running her fingertips over the wood: she had never seen anything as intricate before, apart from the memorial bench that Dad had made. However, the memorial bench could not match the scale of the wall carvings: it must have taken many painstaking months, years even, to complete. Her eyes wandered over every detail, stopping at the top of the carving, near the high ceiling, where the date 1776 was carved into the wood. *What happened in 1776? It must be something to do with Lady Ronan's ancestors,'* she thought. She suddenly remembered seeing the same date displayed on the entrance to Rubbelswick Chambers.

There were so many details to admire: she studied a young girl standing by a dragon, near to a castle. She then noticed that the castle gate, about the size of a large tea mug, had a spring-like movement. She pressed the castle gate several times. *It must open,* she thought excitedly. *What could be behind this door?* Her heart was pounding with excitement as she continued trying to prize open the catch. *It's not budging!* She looked around for something sharp to help her.

She rummaged through writing paper, envelopes, and pens on the writing desk and spotted a letter opener. She picked it up and went back to the carving, where she persevered until the gate popped open.

Lydia couldn't believe her eyes: nestled on a blue velvet cushion was an ornate golden key and a diamond-shaped angel.

Why would they be hidden away in this wood carving? Lydia was puzzled. She studied the key and the angel, baffled and unsure of what to do next.

What if I take them out of the carving and it's a trap? Like some sort of spy movie? she thought. She walked over to the bed where the cats were lying. 'Do you know this carving? You were always with Lady Ronan, and I don't know what to do,' she said quietly. One of the cats stood up, jumped onto the bedside cabinet and began pawing at various items. Lydia looked to see what the cat was pawing at. On the bedside cabinet were several miniature wood carvings; again of a young girl, dragons, angels and fairies, resembling the ones on the wall carving.

'Do you want me to pick this up?' she said, while pointing to the wood carving of a young girl. Suddenly, the cat hit at the carving with its paw, knocking it to the floor.

Lydia picked up the carving and sat on the bed to study it. On the bottom of the carving, there was a small incision: it looked as though something might be inside.

Once again, she ran back to the writing desk, and opened several little drawers to find something small and sharp and smaller than the letter opener.

Paperclips should do it, she thought. Finding one, she straightened it out. Using the clip like a key she patiently picked at the incision until finally a tiny paper scroll fell into the palm of her hand. Delicately, she unrolled the scroll. A verse was written on it:

Hold the angel towards the sun, and all his evil doings will be undone. But a golden key you will need to recover, to unlock a world you are destined to discover.

Lydia kept on repeating the verse over and over in her head, trying to make sense of what it meant. As she sat on the edge of Lady Ronan's bed, she reflected on everything that had happened to her over the past few weeks. Lydia was unsure of what it all meant: the golden key, the Diamond Angel, and now the scroll with the verse inside. She felt a sense of hopelessness, but remembered then what Lady Ronan had told her: 'You're destined for great things'. The cats jumped off the bed and began pawing at her legs. 'What are you doing?' she said, confused by the cat's behaviour.

As Lydia stood up, the cats walked across the bedroom, looking to see if she was following them. They stopped by a large portrait hanging on the wall of a young girl, who resembled Lydia. *It must be either Lady Ronan or one of her ancestors when they were young*, she thought.

Would the painting hold a clue? She began feeling all around the antique frame. As she ran her both hands down the right side of the frame she found a latch; she flicked it up and pulled the heavy portrait towards her. It moved.

'It's a doorway! A doorway! Thank you, cats,' she said, excitedly. She was apprehensive about where the doorway would lead, but that didn't stop her curiosity. She took out the golden key and diamond-shaped angel from the wood carving and placed them on top of the bed. She read the verse on the scroll once more.

'Hold the angel towards the sun, and all his evil doings will be undone.'

There's no sun. I wonder, if I hold the angel towards the lamp, it might work? It's bright enough. Lydia took the Diamond Angel in her left hand and held it between her two fingers towards the lamp, where an inscription was revealed. *There's writing inside the angel, another verse, or maybe a poem.*

She read out the words, etched in gold italics:

Oh, ancient stairs lead me around and around, to where a dark tunnel shall be found. Let the water guide me to a place that I never knew. Turn the key to reveal a veil between two worlds, one waiting to be free. Never worry or be full of fear, for the realm of Veena will hold you near.

The doorway would lead to the stairs: she would have to go through the door, leading perhaps to another part of the castle. Lydia's imagination took over. *What if it's a treasure vault that's*

61

been there for hundreds of years? She couldn't think rationally; she was curious but nervous about where the doorway would take her. Lydia put the golden key, diamond-shaped angel, and the paper scroll into her dressing gown pocket. She took a deep breath and walked through the doorway, her curiosity preventing her from turning back. Shining her torch, she walked along a passage with the cats by her side, keeping her company. She felt safer knowing they were with her. Finally, she came to a stone staircase. *This is it; it must be.*

Oh, ancient stairs lead me around and around.

Slowly, she began descending the round stone staircase, one cat in front of her and the other behind. Round and round, she continued. *How far does this staircase go down?* she thought, as she counted each step *119, 120, 121, 122!* She reached the bottom of the stone staircase at last, and found a stream of water that flowed into a dark tunnel. Lydia came at a halt. She was in the foundations of the castle and couldn't go any lower. She was in the right place, it was in the poem: stone staircase, dark tunnel, water.

Lydia began walking into the dark, damp tunnel, where moss covered the stone walls. It smelt like wet soil. Her only source of light came from her torch. However, halfway into the tunnel, Lydia's torch began flickering. *Oh no, I hope my batteries don't die on me! I won't be able to see anything or make my way back across the castle and back to my bedroom.* Her slippers were sopping wet with the water from the stream and squelched heavily on the ground. With little battery power left in her torch, she had no choice but to abandon her plans of going any further and had to make her way back to Lady Ronan's bedroom.

Before ascending back up the stone staircase, Lydia stared into the dark, watery tunnel and vowed to return the following night. She wanted to know exactly what was lurking in the depths of Gwendonia castle, and where the tunnel would lead her.

*

Lydia was safely back in the confines of Lady Ronan's bedroom. She closed the secret doorway and frantically made her way back to her bedroom as her torch was losing power. Then she remembered: 'The cats! Where are the cats? They must be in the tunnel!' she panicked. She convinced herself that the cats would be fine until she returned there. She crept through the dark passages carrying her soaked slippers, which dripped over the carpets, hardly believing what she had found in the round tower. Mr Rubbelswick was right after all: Gwendonia did appear to be enchanted.

She had done it! She'd made it back to her bedroom without getting caught. Skrinkle was still asleep, oblivious to what she had found in the round tower.

'I missed you, Skrinkle,' she said softly, 'but you are better staying here, where it's safe.' She sat on the edge of her bed and pulled out the golden key and Diamond Angel from her dressing gown pocket.

'What door could this possibly lead to?' she thought anxiously, yet full of excitement. Her thoughts returned to Lady Ronan's cats alone in the damp, dark tunnel: *they're clever cats, they'll be OK,* she convinced herself. After all, they had helped her find the scroll and secret door.

Lydia held the diamond-shaped angel up to her bedroom light, and it sparkled all around the room. Once again, it revealed its hidden golden inscription. While holding the Diamond Angel, Lydia felt a sense of wonder. 'Where have you come from? What do your words mean? I just don't understand,' she sighed. Immediately after, she heard a noise outside her bedroom door. *Maybe it's the cats; they've found their way back.* Lydia hurried to her door and opened it without hesitation, believing that the cats would be outside, but to her disappointment, there was no one there. As she looked up and down the dark passage, she heard the soft voice of a woman echoing in the darkness, 'All will be revealed, all will be revealed, now sleep my child.'

Lydia gasped, and slammed and bolted her bedroom door. She grabbed Skrinkle, jumped into bed and pulled the bedclothes right over her head. She was terrified. 'What was that? Who was that? The longer I live at Gwendonia, the more I believe it's enchanted, Skrinkle.' She cuddled Skrinkle close to her. 'Maybe you were meant to come and protect me . . . but protect me from what?' She began thinking back to the note on Skrinkle's collar: *The one called Skrinkle they will send . . . but* who had sent him? 'I wish you could talk Skrinkle, I really do,' she sighed. Skrinkle buried his head into Lydia's neck, and she felt safer, now that the fox cub was by her side.

Lydia couldn't sleep, however, because she was afraid of the voice she'd heard in the passage. 'I shouldn't be frightened Skrinkle, I love Gwendonia, and Lady Ronan wasn't afraid, living here,' she said, sighing again. Eventually, she fell asleep.

Lydia was woken by repeated knocks on her bedroom door. It was Dad, calling her for breakfast. Still tired from the previous night's adventures, Lydia opened her bedroom door, letting out the biggest yawn.

'Have you slept?' asked Dad.

'Yes, of course, Dad.'

'Didn't you sleep well? You look so tired.'

'No, not really: I kept waking up throughout the night,' she explained, feeling bad about keeping secrets from him. Still, she didn't dare tell him the truth, which was that she had been wandering around the castle in the middle of the night, gone to the round rower and then walked into a mysterious, wet tunnel, and that there was the fox cub hiding in her bedroom. Lydia would have some serious explaining to her parents, so she didn't say a word and kept it all to herself.

As she was making her way down the passage her bother yelled, 'Wait for me!'

'Come on Ellis, hurry!'

Ellis ran towards Lydia, and they began chatting while walking to the kitchen.

'What's wrong with you?' asked Ellis.

'Nothing! Why?'

'Did I hear you last night? I thought I heard voices coming from the passage and your bedroom door opening and slamming.'

'You didn't hear me, you understand? I was sleeping.'

'I was only concerned about you; I was going to check to see if you were OK. Next time, I won't bother!' he snapped then relented. 'You haven't been the same since we moved here and to be honest, I'm getting a little worried about you.'

'I'm fine, really, you don't need to be worried about me. These past weeks have been difficult, with everything that's gone on,' said Lydia, giving her brother a slight smile.

'Do you fancy exploring the round tower? I think I'm going to face my fears today,' he laughed.

'No, I don't want to explore it; stay away from the round tower. You don't like it, so why go?' she exclaimed.

'I can't win with you, can I?' replied Ellis, agitated.

Lydia wanted Ellis to keep as far away from the round tower as possible, in case he found the doorway that led to the stone staircase. A part of her wanted to tell him, but somehow she felt she couldn't.

Lydia had to think of something and fast. 'Let's go explore the dungeons,' she suggested. The dungeons were situated far from the round tower, in a different part of the castle.

'Ok, I bet they're creepy too,' he whined.

'Ellis, we live in a castle that's a thousand years old and parts of it haven't changed for centuries, including the dungeons. Come on, let's go and explore. See what we can find,' Lydia said eagerly.

'What are you two up to today?' asked Gran.

'We're off to explore the dungeons,' said Lydia.

'What if we find skeleton bones, or skulls of prisoners who were tortured and starved to death?' Ellis mocked.

'Oh, Ellis, there are no skeletons in the dungeons. You have such an imagination,' replied Gran, giggling.

'If Ellis found a skeleton in the dungeon, Gran, you'd hear him screaming all the way over here,' Lydia chuckled.

'No, I wouldn't scream—why would I scream? I am older and braver than you, Lydia. I'll keep you safe,' he said confidently.

'Yeah, OK, Ellis, you're older and braver than me. Well, let's go and explore the dungeons, or are you afraid?' she giggled.

'I'm waiting for *you*,' Ellis said assertively.

'Will you two just go and explore this enormous castle,' said Gran.

'See you later, Gran,' they said, kissing her on her cheek before heading off.

Soon, they were standing outside the dungeon gates.

65

'Look, Lyd,' there are spider webs all over the gates. Yuck!' Ellis moaned.

He found a large stick and began scraping off the spider webs. 'You'd think it was Halloween with all these webs everywhere. We're just missing the pumpkins,' he laughed.

'What are you blabbering about Ellis?

'Spiders' webs? Pumpkins? Get it?

'Yeah, I get it. Just scrape off the webs with your stick,' replied Lydia.

'What do you think I'm doing?

'Don't start, or else you'll be going in the dungeons on your own,' said Lydia.

'Looks as though no one has been here for years,' said Ellis.

'You're probably right. God knows what we'll find in there.'

Once Ellis had scraped off all the spider webs he looked around to Lydia, who was standing behind him, and asked her if was she was ready to explore the dungeons.

'Let's go,' she replied.

There were no locks on the dungeon gate so they pushed the creaky gate as hard as they could until it opened.

'Come on, let's see what's inside here,' Ellis said excitedly.

It was dark and smelt of damp earth. It was the same smell that Lydia had smelt when she was in the tunnel the previous night.

'Follow me closely, Lydia,' said Ellis, while taking his torch from his pocket.

He began shining the torch towards the dungeon ceiling. 'Look up there-what are they?' he said, puzzled.

Hanging from the dungeon ceilings were large, rusted steel brackets. Hanging on the end of each bracket were round, iron cages.

'I told you didn't I? I bet they were used to torture people,' Ellis said, smugly.

'We don't know what they are. They could have been used for anything,' said Lydia.

Lydia and Ellis walked further into the dungeon, feeling nervous because they didn't know what might be lurking in the darkness. Suddenly, they heard a scuttling sound.

'Who's there?' Ellis shouted out, while clinging on to Lydia.
'Who's there? I demand you tell me who you are!'

'It's probably rats,' hissed Lydia.

'Rats? Rats? In the castle dungeons?' said Ellis, panicked.

'Oh, for goodness' sake, Ellis, I don't know if the noise we heard was rats. It could be anything. After all, there is no lock on the gate. Perhaps some sort of wildlife has made its home here,' said Lydia.

'Now stop being a wuss, will you? After all, you're older and braver than me, aren't you Ellis?' she giggled.

'Shut up, Lydia. Let's find out where the noise was coming from,' he scowled.

He pointed his torch towards the ceiling and slowly began looking for any sign of animals that might have made the scuttling noise, while Lydia studied the floor for any signs that woodland animals.

Ellis started to tap his torch on the dungeon walls and disturbed a colony of bats. 'Argh! Argh! Get off! Get off!!' he yelled, flapping his hands as the bats flew around his head, trying to keep them away.

Lydia was fits of laughter at her brother. 'That's brilliant,'' she mocked, as she mimicked his frantic flapping.

'Is that all you can do? Laugh? They just startled me, that's all,' said Ellis, feeling embarrassed again.

'Well, we haven't found any skeletons, just bats,' she continued to giggle.

'Lydia, shhh, be quiet. Can you hear that noise?' said Ellis.

They stood still and once more heard the same scuttling sound.

'It's like something is running away from us,' said Lydia, looking at her brother.

'Told you, didn't I?'

'What do you think it is?' she asked nervously.

'It sounds like running feet.'

'Who's there? We can hear you, you know,' called out Lydia.

The sound of muffled voices could be heard, as though someone was having a conversation.

'I don't want to be down here anymore,' Ellis said, startled at what he was hearing.

'Ellis, you wanted to explore the castle. Well, guess what? That's exactly what we are doing,' said Lydia sternly.

'Fancy exploring the round tower instead?' he nervously giggled.

'No! We are not exploring the round tower. We are in the dungeons, Ellis, and that's what we are going to explore,' said Lydia.

There was no light except for Ellis's torch. 'Quickly, pass me the torch Ellis,' Lydia asked impatiently.

'Why?'

'Will you just give it to me?'

Ellis reluctantly passed Lydia his torch.

'Look at the walls, look, do you see Ellis? They're all the way along the bottom of the walls.'

'Oh yeah, but what are they?' he asked, squinting at lots of little arched iron doors, no more than a foot high. Lydia crouched down, opened one of the doors, and shone the torch into it.

'The hole goes right back; there don't appear to be any walls,' she whispered.

Ellis and Lydia looked through all the other arched doors, but they were all empty.

'I have no idea what they are—I'm totally baffled,' said Ellis.

Lydia shook her head, thinking that the castle was getting stranger by the day.

'When we next come to the dungeons, I'll bring my torch and we'll have more light,' said Lydia.

'I am not coming down here again, not a chance. It's weird. All those mysterious tiny doorways: where do they lead?' said Ellis.

'I have no idea.''

A creaking noise came out of the darkness.

'That sounds like one of the little iron gates opening. Come on Ellis, let's go and look,' said Lydia, dragging her brother by the arm.

'Look there's one open—the sound must have come from there. Someone or *something* opened it.' She shone the torch through the small doorway, but could see nothing. The hole was empty.

'Perhaps the wind opened it,' said Ellis.

68

'Wind? We're in a dungeon,' replied Lydia.

'Well, if there is a tunnel on the other side, perhaps there is wind blowing. Oh well, I don't know what it is or what caused it.'

'Lydia? Ellis? Are you in there?' It was Gran calling them, her voice echoing through the tunnel.

'We'd better go back,' said Ellis.

'OK,' agreed Lydia.

As they made their way towards the dungeon entrance, Lydia had an overwhelming feeling that something was watching them. She turned around quickly and shone the torch back into the dungeon, while pointing the torch towards the little iron gates.

'Ellis, did you see it? Did you?' said Lydia nervously.

'See what?'

'It looked like a little person, standing by the opened gate. Like an elf or something, looking straight at us' she said frantically.

'Elf? You had me then, good one. I'll get you back. You wait and see,' he laughed.

'It was real, it was so tiny; like something you see in a fairy-tale book.'

'It's most likely a badger,' he giggled.

'A badger? I know what a badger looks like! It was not a badger. It was a person, I'm certain!' she proclaimed.

'I'd stick with the possibility of it being a badger if I were you; you sound completely mad. Why would little people or elves be in the dungeon?' he scoffed.

Lydia knew that what she was telling her brother seemed impossible to believe. However, she knew what she had seen, and never in her life, nor in the depths of the most enchanting fairy-tale book, had she seen anything quite like it.

Back at the entrance of the dungeon, they met Gran and Ellis walked back to the castle with her, while Lydia dawdled at the dungeon gate. As she gazed into the dark abyss it appeared that it wasn't only the round tower that held secrets: the dungeon had theirs, too.

'I'll find out exactly what I saw today when I return to the round tower tonight,' she vowed, desperate to solve the castle's many riddles.

Chapter 7

Entering The Realm

It was midnight and Lydia was sitting on the edge of her bed, dressed and prepared, waiting patiently to return to the round tower. She crept out of the bedroom, confident that all her family were asleep. She had the same feeling of anxiousness, coupled with excitement, whirling around in her head. All her thoughts were concentrating on what was in the tunnel. Would she see the cats? Would she see small iron arched doors, like those in the castle dungeons? Once more, she was at Lady Ronan's bedroom. She opened the door, closed it behind her, and switched on the bedside lamp. She looked around, hoping to see Lady Ronan's cats, but they were nowhere to be seen. Where could they have gone? Lydia had no clue of their whereabouts and was concerned that they might be trapped in the tunnel.

Before venturing down the stone staircase, Lydia ensured that she had everything with her, emptying the contents of her bag onto Lady Ronan's bed to double-check: torch, spare batteries, the golden key, the diamond-shaped angel, the Lamanya Stone. Everything was there.

Lydia sighed heavily and once more made her way to the secret doorway. With both hands she pulled open the heavy door until the gap was big enough for her to squeeze through.

Here we go, she thought to herself, and slowly descended the spiral stone staircase. Soon, she found herself back in the black, watery tunnel.

The stream flowed into the abyss of the dark tunnel. Lydia looked down at her water-resistant black ankle boots. *No soggy slippers for me tonight*, she thought. She was wearing navy-blue jeans and a lemon-coloured woollen jumper to ensure that she kept warm, as the tunnel was cold and damp. She shone the torch into the tunnel, and began following the stream. Apart from the

70

noise of running water, there was no other sound; just her footsteps echoing with every step she took.

Lydia continued further and deeper into the tunnel. 'Cats! Cats! Are you here?' Her voice echoed through the tunnel. Where could they be? She walked for a considerable time and soon she realised that she was deep into the tunnel.

'There's nothing here; not even the cats,' she said aloud, frustrated.

Suddenly, over the sound of the running water, she could hear something: *Meow! Meow! Meow!* 'Cats, is it you? Please be you!' she called out. And then, caught in the torchlight, standing silently, were Lady Ronan's black cats. 'Ahh, there you are. I thought I'd lost you. What on earth is down here?' she said, while affectionately stroking each cat.

'Come on, let's go back. There is nothing here,' she said, disappointed. As Lydia started to make her way back out of the tunnel, she expected the cats to follow her. However, when she looked back, she saw that the cats were strolling further into the tunnel. 'Why won't you come with me? There's nothing here. You can't stay down here,' she insisted. The cats dismissed Lydia's pleas, which she found this quite odd. 'You want me to follow you, do you?'

She paused for a moment then began running towards the cats. 'Wait for me! I hope you know where you're going!'

The cats walked either side of Lydia as they descended further down the tunnel, Lydia's torch lighting the way. After a while, Lydia became frustrated again. 'This is totally pointless. I'm going back. I'm not going any further. Apart from the stream, there's nothing here,' she said. One of the cats pawed at her leg. 'What? What's wrong?' she asked. The torchlight caught something gleaming in the distance. Squinting her eyes, Lydia tried to make out what could it be, her heart racing and pounding rapidly all the while. She felt that she needed to compose herself and took several deep breaths to try to normalise her breathing. The once flowing stream that had led Lydia through the tunnel was now trickling into a large, shallow pond, which lay before the mysterious, glistening object.

'It's a door!' she exclaimed, looking down at the two cats at her side. The door was enormous, arched and golden; Lydia could not comprehend its size; she had never seen anything like it.

Images of castles, dragons, and fairies were engraved into its surface, just like those on the wood carving in Lady Ronan's bedroom. The images on the door appeared to be moving, like the figures displayed on a zoetrope to produce the illusion of motion. Lydia was mesmerised and couldn't take her eyes off the moving pictures.

The door was at least 20ft high, with a keyhole at the bottom left corner. Lydia quickly rummaged into her bag and took out the golden key, remembering the inscription revealed within the angel-shaped diamond.

Turn the key to reveal a veil between two worlds, one waiting to be free.

Repeating the same sentence in her head, she tried the lock with the key, her hands shaking with apprehension. She couldn't turn back, not now. *It has to fit, it just has to*, she thought, as she placed the key into the keyhole and began turning it slowly. Would she find an explanation for what had been happening over a bizarre couple of weeks? With her heart racing, she kept turning the key: *Click, click, click, click.* 'Oh, why isn't it opening?' she cried.

The cats were looking back into the dark tunnel. 'Oh no, who's coming? What can you see?' she said, petrified. She could hear the sound of running feet. Lydia froze. *I'm going to die in this tunnel, and no one will find me.* She was in a total panic but summoned all her courage and called out, 'Who's there? Who are you?' Suddenly, she heard gekkering, the sort of sound made by foxes, getting louder and louder. Skrinkle running towards her, his fur all wet from running through the stream of water.

'Oh, Skrinkle, you frightened me. What are you doing here? How did you get out of my bedroom and find me?' She quickly picked him up and cuddled him.

'You poor thing, you've walked all the way here just to find me. I do love you, Skrinkle,' she whispered in his ear.

'I love you too, Lydia,' replied Skrinkle.

'Wh-what?' She almost dropped him into the water. She put him down and stepped back from him, too traumatised to speak. Keeping her distance, she summoned the courage to address him.

'I, I, heard you talk, didn't I? I'm not imagining it. I heard you talk. I'm not losing my mind. But you're a fox cub. Foxes aren't supposed to talk, like humans. You're supposed to just speak in fox language, to other foxes,' she babbled. Skrinkle looked up at her. 'I don't want to frighten you, and I certainly would never harm you. But I'm going to spin around, fast, as though I'm chasing my bushy tail,' he giggled.

'Spin around fast? What's going on?' demanded Lydia. With that, Skrinkle began spinning around in a clockwise motion, extremely fast, just as if he were chasing his tail. Lydia was in shock and leant against the tunnel wall, breathing fast. She wanted to run, and couldn't believe what she was witnessing. There were all sorts of bright colours radiating from Skrinkle as he continued to spin, around and around. When he stopped, he had fully transformed into a three-foot adult fox, standing up straight and walking on his two back paws. He had the gentlest voice and spoke very eloquently. 'Hello little one, I'm Skrinkle.' Lydia was frozen to the spot, speechless.

'I didn't mean to startle you,' he reassured her. Lydia stared back: he certainly looked like a fox, with his orange and white fur, but he was wearing a navy military-style coat studded with eight brass buttons and a black leather belt around his waist, hanging from which was a a jewel-encrusted dagger. Finally, Lydia managed to get her words out.

'Who are you?'

'It's me, Skrinkle. Since the cats brought me to your bedroom, I've taken care of you,' he replied.

'I don't understand; what is going on?' said Lydia.

'My name is Skrinkle, the fox cub,' he replied.

'Yes, I'm aware that your name is Skrinkle. I've been looking after you for days in my bedroom,' she snapped. 'How can you talk? What's going on? You need to tell me; otherwise, I'll get my father and grandfather and tell them everything that's happened. Do you understand? Since moving into Gwendonia, I've seen statutes move and a pixie or an elf in the dungeon peeping out at me from a little arched doorway. I expect to find them in a fairy-tale book, not in the depths of the castle foundations.'

'I'm not from a fairy book. I am standing in front of you, having just transformed in front of your very eyes, have I not?' replied Skrinkle.

Lydia didn't know what to say. The truth was, she didn't have a logical answer to what she had witnessed. It certainly made her think that the castle was truly enchanted.

'I'm sorry for snapping at you, but it's all a bit bizarre, ' Lydia explained. 'So, was it a pixie that I saw?' she asked.

'Not a pixie, I'm afraid. You saw a male Woodilf. They're quite cute little beings. The Woodilf are from the enchanted forest, just behind your house, and many of them have lived here in the castle dungeons for centuries. They're known as sentry folk, because they guard the castle against evil, alongside the Asiras. But you mustn't ever compare them to pixies; never. They don't like to be compared. You see, they are the Woodilfs and very proud of that fact. They are not pixies, or elves, or goblins, or fairies. Do you see where I'm going with this? You call them Wood-ilfs,' said Skrinkle, assertively.

'What are you talking about? This isn't a normal conversation,' said Lydia.

'What is normal, Lydia? We are alive, just like you, but from a different realm, which happens to be in the foundations of Gwendonia castle,' replied Skrinkle, with a little chuckle.

'Realm? What do you mean?'

'You cannot tell anyone. Please trust me; all will be revealed when you open the golden door,' said Skrinkle.

'You expect me to open the door after you just transformed into an adult fox? What else is behind there? An enchanted world?' scoffed Lydia.

'Well, yes, if you put it like that. It's called Veena, and it is the most breathtaking place you'll ever see. But I'll let you decide that for yourself,' said Skrinkle. 'You're meant to open the door, Lydia. You've found the key, remember?'

'I have to admit that I'm a little afraid to open the door,' Lydia confessed.

'You have nothing to fear, little one. You are brave and have so much strength deep within you. Everyone in Veena is so eager to meet you,' continued Skrinkle excitedly. 'Trust me, all will be revealed as soon as you enter Veena. All the strange events that you have experienced will all make sense, I promise.'

'What if I die once I open the door? My father will eventually find you all, remember that,' said Lydia. She was rather scared.

'Oh Lydia, you are not going to die; everyone is expecting your arrival,' Skrinkle reassured her.

'You promise I'll come back in one piece? I'm leaving for Ireland in several hours. At 11am, in fact, to visit my grandparents, and it's already 2.40am!' cried Lydia.

'I promise, just open the door, and I'll make sure you're back in time for your trip,' said Skrinkle.

Lydia turned the key clockwise again: *Click, click, click.* 'Is it open now?' Lydia asked.

'Stand back, Lydia,' said Skrinkle, as he pushed open the heavy golden door with both paws. Lydia tried to peek over Skrinkle's shoulder to see what was on the other side. Brilliant light spilled through the opened door, illuminating up the tunnel. Once the door had opened, Skrinkle stepped through and turned to Lydia. 'There! Isn't it the most beautiful place you have ever seen?' he smiled. Lydia slowly stepped forward and stood by the entrance looking into another world, taking in its beauty.

'I can't believe what I'm seeing,' she gasped, 'an enchanted world, under our castle . . . I . . . I have no words.'

Skrinkle held out a paw. 'Come, Lydia, let me show you the wonderment of Veena. You'll never want to leave,' he smiled. Slowly, reluctantly, but with an overwhelming feeling of excitement, she held out her hand and stepped into Veena. Suddenly, they were joined by the two cats.

'No cats, you can't come. Please stay in the tunnel,' she pleaded.

'All is not what it seems, Lydia,' said Skrinkle. Immediately, both cats started bounding across the meadow. With a blast of the brightest of white lights, they too had transformed into two massive white tigers. 'Tigers! Lady Ronan's cats!' she gasped.

Skrinkle laughed, 'No, they are certainly not house cats. They are the Harimau tigers, who live in Veena. They were disguised as black cats when they brought me to you, remember?' he smiled.

'Yes, I do,' she smiled back. 'Why are they at Gwendonia?'

75

'They are protectors. They guard the castle too, and they also kept Lady Ronan safe all her life,' he explained.

'Safe? Safe from what?'

'There are so many questions that you seek answers to, Lydia, but all will be revealed shortly,' he replied.

They began walking across the meadow. Lydia stared at the landscape in awe: there were waterfalls, lakes, meadows brimming with wildflowers that popped and peeked out of the luscious, long green grass in bursts of colour.

'What are those things in the grass?' she said, pointing towards glittering little platforms, about two feet in height, which peppered the meadow.

'They are the plinths for the Tulwen fairies and Hafli elves to rest on, so they don't get lost in the grass,' Skrinkle chuckled. Each plinth bore intricate carvings of enchanted creatures, with a letter V, for Veena, right at the top.

'Tulwen fairies? Hafli elves? I don't understand what is going on, Skrinkle. Who are they?'

'I know it's overwhelming for you, but all will be transparent soon enough,' he replied. 'I'm sure you'll become extremely fond of the Tulwens and Haflis. They are simply lovely little folk,' Skrinkle gushed.

'Yes, I'm sure I will,' replied Lydia, still trying to make sense of what she was seeing and what was happening to her. As they walked, Skrinkle told her more about Veena. Lydia noticed several large objects shining brightly and moving slowly, close to a waterfall. The brightness was so powerful that Lydia had to put her hand up towards her eyes.

'What are those shining objects, Skrinkle?' asked Lydia.

'I knew you'd notice,' he smiled, 'They're the Duons.'

'Duons?'

'Yes, the Duon dragonflies. There are many of them here. The Veronians fly them all over Veena,' he explained.

'What is a Veronian?' she asked.

'They are the people who live here,' he replied. 'Let's go and introduce you to the Duons!'

As Lydia walked closer,' the Duons seemed to grow larger and larger. 'They are ever so big, Skrinkle,' she said.

They were huge in fact; she had never seen such a sight. The only dragonflies Lydia had seen before were the ones at the pond at home. These dragonflies, however, were gigantic! They had pretty, round faces, and large, round, black eyes that glittered. They were all sorts of colours, too: some were blue, others yellow, green, orange, and purple. As their massive, glistening wings stretched out; they were indeed a magnificent sight to behold.

'Are they friendly?' asked Lydia.

'The friendliest, but in battle, they can be ferocious. Well, they would be, wouldn't they? When it comes to protecting Veena. It's our home Lydia.' said Skrinkle.

'Whatever do you mean? What battle?' asked Lydia.

'They are part of our army. There has been a battle here in Veena,' replied Skrinkle, looking rather upset.

Lydia began stroking one of the Duons. She could not comprehend why a magical place like Veena would require an army.

'Skrinkle, may I ask you a question?' she said.

'Yes, fire away.'

'This place is enchanted, isn't it? Everything that I'm seeing and feeling is real, isn't it? I'm not in a bizarre dream, am I?'

'No, you're definitely not in a dream-like state. This is completely real and enchanted. Well, I'll let you make up your own mind once I've taken you around Veena,' smiled Skrinkle, as he climbed onto one of the Duons.

'What are you doing?'

'I'm taking you around Veena! It's a big place, with so much to see. That's why we need to fly. Hop on one of the Duons, Lydia! It's perfectly safe. They are marvellous flyers,' he said excitedly, ready to take to the air. Lydia clumsily climbed on the Duon and made herself comfortable.

'Right, you need to take hold of its collar and hold onto it tightly, and when you are ready, we'll take off together,' said Skrinkle.

'Don't leave without me. Promise you'll stay by my side?' she asked in a panicked voice.

'Little one, I won't leave you, not for a minute,' he reassured her. 'One, two, three, Duons fly! Duons fly!' called out Skrinkle.

The Duons rose up into the air like helicopters and soared upwards, with Skrinkle and Lydia flying next to one another.

'It's even more breathtaking up here,' shouted Lydia. 'Who lives there?' She pointed to a quaint little castle situated at the edge of a forest.

'The Tulwen fairies! I'll take you to meet them later, and then you'll meet the Hafli elves, who don't live far from Tulwen castle. They, too, have the loveliest of houses nestled away in the Hafeena forest. I think you'll love the Tulwens and Haflis,' said Skrinkle.

'I'm sure I will. I've never met a real fairy or elf before; they have always come to life in my imagination when reading books,' she smiled.

'There are hundreds of fairies and elves here in Veena—that I can guarantee!' he beamed.

Lydia was so excited she could hardly wait to meet them. However, she was enjoying seeing Veena from the air, which spread out below them for mile after mile. She could hardly contain herself that she was in an enchanted world: this was not in her imagination; this was REAL. She felt highly privileged to be a part of it all.

'Look, Lydia! That's where the Veronians live,' said Skrinkle, pointing towards the ground.

The Veronians spotted Skrinkle and Lydia in the sky and began smiling and waving up at them enthusiastically.

'They seem so friendly,' Lydia enthused.

'They are, and you'll get to meet them eventually; you'll meet everyone in Veena,' he told her.

Lydia smiled and waved back as they continued to soar across the sky.

BANG! BANG! BANG! Clank! Clank! The noise was deafening. Lydia tried to cover her ears but had to hold onto the Duon too. 'What's that noise? My ears are going to burst!' she shouted to Skrinkle.

'Don't be alarmed. We are flying over the mountains where the Spoglys live,' he replied.

'Spoggys? What are Spoggys?' yelled Lydia over the piercing noise.

'No, not Spoggys—Spoglys,' he repeated.

'I get it, Spoglys, but what are they?'

'They are giants who live inside the mountains of Veena.'

'You have giants? Actual giants?'

'Yes, lots of them. Come, let's go and meet them.'

In the distance, Lydia could see a wooden door of colossal size placed in the middle of an enormous mountain. She had never seen anything as big; not even the majestic Gwendonia could match its size.

'See the door embedded into the mountain? That's the entrance to where they live. Let's get closer and say hello,' he suggested.

Lydia was terrified. 'What if the Spoglys don't like me? And I end up in soup or something?'

'I think you been reading too many fairy-tale books, Lydia. They would never harm you, never. They are looking forward to meeting you.' As they flew closer to the mountains, the noise of banging and clanking grew louder, reverberating all over Veena.

'I can't believe what I'm seeing! Look Skrinkle! Look!' she yelled, 'It's, it's a giant . . . a giant, an actual giant!'

The giant was 60ft tall, with dishevelled dark-brown hair, of human-like appearance, with a complexion tinged pale green, and big, brown eyes. The giant wore a beige linen tabard and matching three-quarter length trousers, while his gigantic feet and hairy toes poked through his enormous leather strap sandals. Lydia and Skrinkle were hovering over the giants' head.

'Yes, he is a giant,' chuckled Skrinkle. Lydia peered past the giant's head and gazed into his home. There was a chair, which resembled scaffolding. On the chair was a chocolate-brown cushion the size of a very large sofa! There was a wooden table so high that it would have required several ladders for an average person to reach the top of it. On the table were plates and goblets made from shiny metal, and huge chunks of half-eaten stale bread on the most enormous stone platter. The scraps of bread bore huge teeth marks that the giant had made, preserving the impression of his teeth like a fossil.

'Uze! Uze, please, will you stop banging!' yelled Skrinkle.

Uze's voice was loud and raspy. 'Ah, Skrinkle, hello me old friend! Good to see you back in Veena.' He dropped down his enormous hammer, *THUD*, and it bounced onto the ground below.

'This is Uze, is Miss Lydia,' said Skrinkle.

Uze bowed his head to Lydia as if he were honoured to meet her. 'Welcome to Veena.'

'Thank you, Uze,' but there is no need to bow to me. I'm just an ordinary girl, nothing special or regal about me.'

'You be special to us in Veena, Miss Lydia,' he replied, his voice loud and raspy.

'Well, thank you again, Uze, that is very kind of you to say,' said Lydia.

'Whatever are you making, Uze? You could hear the noise over the other end of Veena,' said Skrinkle.

'Me making weapons, of course, to fight that evil Ballam, should he ever return . I be prepared for him. I'll rip off his wings and tear off his head, so me do. He is evil, pure and simple, Miss Lydia,' said Uze.

'I don't know who Ballam is, sorry Uze,' she replied. 'Who is he, Skrinkle?' she whispered.

'You mean she never knows who Ballam is, Skrinkle? What's all this? She needs to know, doesn't she? She the one helping us ain't she, my friend? You haven't told her yet?' Uze ranted. He looked at Lydia and quickly apologized. 'Oh, Uze is so sorry. Me don't think before I speak. Me have always been the same, ain't I, Skrink?'

'It's OK, not to worry. It's not your fault, Uze,' replied Skrinkle. 'Lydia will know all about Ballam before she leaves Veena; she will know everything.'

'I feel as if I have a right to know who this Ballam is, especially as Uze believes I'm going to help Veena,' responded Lydia in an icy tone.

'I'm sorry, Lydia. Perhaps I should have told you, but it's not my place, you see. I felt it would be better to tell you, here in Veena. Where it'll make sense once you meet everyone. It's why Lady Ronan believed in you; she believed that you could help us,' he replied.

'OK, I think I understand, but no more keeping things from me: I need to know everything. I mean everything, Skrinkle,' said Lydia.

'Yup, me old friend,' said Uze, 'she be right. She needs to know the truth about Veena.'

'I know, and she'll know soon enough,' said Skrinkle.

'Where's your family? And the rest of the Spoglys, Uze?'

'They be in the mountains. Something is going on. We be sure of it. They've gone to check no one has entered Veena. I mean the Sinaras, Skrinkle, that's what I mean,' Uze explained, staring down at his sandals and looking melancholy.

'I know all too well who you are referring to, unfortunately,' replied Skrinkle, looking slightly on edge. Skrinkle turned to Lydia. 'The Sinaras are Ballam's servants, or followers. They're just as evil and destructive as their master.' He shuddered.

'You be right there Skrink, they killed many here in Veena. When Ballam and them tried to destroy us, me never forget that. If I see any of them, just one, I'll kill them. They'll be dead for sure,' said Uze, becoming frustrated at the very thought of them.

'Uze, I'm sorry, truly sorry that you lost members of your family in that awful battle,' said Skrinkle. He leant over and started to pat Uze's shoulder to comfort him.

'Thank you, Skrink. I know that be a long time ago, but me never stop thinking about them, see. They be inside here forever,' he said, pounding his fist several times on his chest, near his heart.

'Your family were courageous and saved many lives by sacrificing their own, and you should be very proud and honoured Uze,' said Skrinkle. 'Remember our motto: *Every beating heart in Veena is the purest and kindest of all hearts.* He can never take that away from us, Uze. We'll never be like him or his servants,' he added.

It was clear to Lydia from this conversation that it was important for Veena to have its army and Duon dragonflies, but she didn't entirely understand what had occurred in Veena and became uneasy about what may be in store for her there.

'We'd best get off. I need to take Lydia to meet the Tulwens and Haflis, and leave you to get back to your weapons; I've kept you far too long,' said Skrinkle.

'It's been lovely meeting you, Miss Lydia. Welcome to Veena, this is your home too,' said Uze.

81

'Thank you, Uze. It was very lovely to meet you too, and I'll be sure to revisit you soon,' Lydia replied.

Uze suddenly let out the biggest and loudest of all sneezes. *Ahchoo! Ahchoo!* The Duons gave out the loudest of screeches as Uze covered them all, along with Lydia and Skrinke, from head to foot in snot. Both Lydia and Skrinkle were speechless and just looked at one another.

'Yuk! Yuk! Uze, that's disgusting. What have you done?' yelled Lydia, her long hair sticking to her head as though she had just stepped out of a shower.

'Me so sorry. It's me hayfever, it's a terrible condition to have, you see,' replied Uze sheepishly, while continuing to wipe his huge, snotty nostrils with his hairy arms.

'Well, you could have warned us,' said Skrinkle,' while shaking and wiping the snot off his face and clothes.

'No time, it came on me suddenly. Me can't control it. Sorry about that.'

Lydia looked at Skrinkle, whose fur was now all congealed and matted. He looked very displeased, so much in fact that she couldn't contain herself and began to laugh hysterically.

'What are you laughing at, Lydia?' asked Skrinkle

'You, Skrinkle, just look at us. We both look so stupid, covered in head to toe in giant's snot!' she laughed.

'Yes, I suppose we do,' chuckled Skrinkle, 'Let's go and wash it off before it dries.'

'Where?' asked Lydia.

'You'll see.''

'Bye Uze,' they shouted, waving to him as they rose up into Veena's sky.

'Sorry, Skrink. Sorry, Lydia,' Uze bellowed, his apology echoing all around the mountains.

'I can't meet the fairies and elves like this Skrinkle. Look at the state of me,' said Lydia.

'Don't worry. You'll be back to your normal self once we get you to the waterfalls.'

Soon, the Duons reached the most captivating waterfall that cascaded down the rocks and into a lagoon below.

'Oh, it's beautiful,' gasped Lydia.

'It is, and we are going straight through it,' said Skrinkle.

'What, through the waterfall?' she asked.

'Yes, that's exactly what I mean,' said Skrinkle excitedly. Slowly, the Duons flew into the waterfall and began to hover, allowing the flowing water to clean all the snot off them all.

'This is fantastic!' yelled Lydia, as she squeezed her hair and held her face up against the flowing water. She felt clean and refreshed and was looking forward to meeting the little beings in Veena. Skrinkle's fur was clean and fluffy and back to normal. There were no knots and not a trace of snot! The Duons flew fast across the sky, and soon Lydia and Skrinkle were completely dried by the warm breeze. The Duons landed and Lydia and Skrinkle found themselves at the edge of the forest. They walked along a cobbled stone path, which led to Tulwen castle.

'Here we are, right outside the castle gate,' said Skrinkle.

Lydia looked up at the castle. It was enchanting, with four fairy-tale turrets covered in pale-green tiles. A sign carved in stone just above the entrance gate announced *TULWEN CASTLE*. Suddenly, the gate opened and they both walked in.

'Skrinkle, there are fairies everywhere!' Lydia gasped. The castle courtyard was full of fairies; Lydia was afraid to move just in case she stood on one of them. The fairies were bigger than she thought they would be, about a foot high and not minuscule at all. They had beautiful faces and small, transparent wings on their backs.

Skrinkle summoned them all. Soon, the castle courtyard was bursting at the seams, with fairies hanging out of the castle windows and the battlements too, just to get a look at Skrinkle and Lydia.

'Hello Tulwens, I have brought Miss Lydia to meet you all. Please welcome her to Veena,' shouted out Skrinkle, smiling. The fairies began jumping and dancing around enthusiastically.

'Hello Miss Lydia! Hello! The Tulwens welcome you to Veena,' they shouted.

Lydia was overwhelmed by what she saw and stood in amazement for several minutes, taking in the wonder of it all. 'Thank you all for such a warm welcome. I'm flattered, truly I am. You have the loveliest castle, and I'm very honoured to meet you all,' she said, with the brightest of smiles.

She noticed that Skrinkle appeared to be looking for something, or someone, in the vast crowd. 'Why no Tint or Wilken? Where are they?' Skrinkle cried. The Tulwens went quiet and looked at each other. A soft voice rose out of the crowd; it was a male fairy, 'They're in the forest, training. They are always and preparing for battle, Skrinkle.'

'Please, can someone fetch them? I need to speak with them. I need to tell you all something important,' said Skrinkle. A few of the Tulwen fairies made their way into the forest.

'Who are Tint and Wilken, Skrinkle?' asked Lydia.

'They're the leaders of the Tulwen fairies, Lydia.'

What did Skrinkle have to tell them, she wondered? 'Look, it's Tint and Wilken!' shouted out one of the fairies, and pointed to two figures flying over the battlements. A moment later, the two Tulwen leaders had landed in the middle of the courtyard.

'Hello Tint, hello Wilken. Wonderful to see you,' smiled Skrinkle.

'Skrinkle, you're back! It's lovely that you have returned to Veena. We have missed you so,' cried Tint.

'Thank you Tint, I have missed you all too, more than you know, but you all know the reasons why I had to leave Veena for a while,' he continued.

'Yes, we know,' replied Tint, looking glum. Lydia watched as the Tulwen leaders talked.

'Tint Tawney and Wilken Pixley, this is the Miss Lydia,' said Skrinkle at last, with his paw resting on her shoulder.

'Hello Tint and Wilken, I'm Lydia, and I come from the earth plane. I was brought here to Veena to meet you all,' she smiled. Lydia had the most infectious of smiles and could light up a room, making everyone feel special, or so she thought.

'You are so cute, just cute!' she cried, directing her comments to Tint and Wilken. Skrinkle rolled his eyes and muttered, 'Here we go,' shaking his head as he waited for Tint to respond.

Tint was furious. 'Cute? I'm not cute at all. I'm a warrior fairy and leader of the Tulwens,' she scowled. Tint quickly took out the littlest of swords from her belt and began waving it about as if she were in battle. Lydia and Skrinkle giggled.

'Tint, what are you doing? That's no way to treat our guest, is it?' said Skrinkle, dodging Tint's sword.

'Tint, I'm sorry! I didn't mean to offend you. I should have said that you are very beautiful and courageous, not cute,' said Lydia.

'Now that's better,' she replied. Her head held high, she flicked her long black hair. In fact, Tint was extremely cute: her little flapping wings; long, straight, fringed black hair; and violet-coloured eyes proved that point. She had a bow and arrow strapped across her chest and a black belt around her waist with a sword dangling from it.

'Tint, stop being so horrible to Lydia,' said Wilken.

'I'm not horrible, Wilken! I just don't like being called cute, that's all. Being called beautiful, however, is another thing,' she replied, smiling.

'Oh, for goodness' sake, Tint, just stop it will you,' Wilken snapped.

'Just because *you* think Lydia is beautiful! You haven't stopped staring at her, have you, Wilken?' said Tint, sounding jealous, and with her arms folded and her eyes closed.

'She is a guest here; treat her like one. We are all pleased she has come here to help us all. Otherwise Veena could be destroyed, don't you understand?' said Wilken.

Lydia bent down and whispered into Tint's ear. 'Shall we start again? Hello, I'm Lydia, and I'm so pleased to meet you.'

Tint had a slight smirk on her face. 'Hello, Lydia, I'm Tint Tawney, leader of the Tulwen fairies, and it's certainly a pleasure to meet you,' she said, giggling. Skrinkle and Wilken looked at one another and shook their heads. Lydia had a calming way about her and seemed to know the right thing to say and do. Lydia's charms worked, for though Tint was a fiery and fierce warrior fairy, she and Lydia began laughing and chatting away as though they were the best of friends and had known each other for years.

Skrinkle spoke to the fairies and told them that Lydia was the chosen one. She would help Veena defeat the evil Ballam by trying to locate the two missing Diamond Angel amulets of the Lamanya plinth.

'Lydia will soon meet the great and wise Zavantos,' Skrinkle told the fairies. Every Tulwen fairy clapped and danced around happily while shouting out, 'Lydia! Lydia! Lydia!'

Lydia looked at Skrinkle. 'Help defeat Ballam? Lamanya plinth? Meet the great Zavantos? Who is that?' she asked eagerly. 'Skrinkle, you really have a lot of explaining to do before I return home.'

'Little one, I know I do,' replied Skrinkle.

'Well,' why don't you just tell me now?'

'Not yet. I'm taking you to meet the Hafli elves. Then you'll meet Zavantos, or Z, as we call him, and he will explain everything to you, I promise.

Skrinkle and Lydia said their goodbyes to the Tulwen fairies and told them that she would return soon. 'Bye Lydia!' shouted out Tint and Wilken from the castle battlements.

'Bye!' Lydia shouted back, waving until the Tulwens were out of sight.

Lydia and Skrinkle returned to the edge of the forest. 'Do you want to meet the Hafli elves? asked Skrinkle. 'Yes, I can't wait,' replied Lydia excitedly.

'We need to take this path,' said Skrinkle, as he pointed the way to Lydia. 'The Duons will have to wait here for us; they can't take us into the woods. We'll have to walk, as there are too many trees and the forest is dense with vegetation. The paths will take us deep into the forest until we reach the Hafeena village.'

'Is it something like a maze?' asked Lydia.

'Yes, I suppose so. There are several paths with its twists and turns, so yes, it's like a maze,' he giggled. 'To get there is somewhat difficult, but then this keeps the Hafli safe from evil. Even the smallest of elves needs to keep safe from the likes of Ballam and his servants. But believe it or not, as little as they are, they are very powerful and can inflict great harm on the evil one, so he always tried to find and destroy them.'

'That's awful. Why is Ballam so evil?' asked Lydia.

'Why is anyone evil? Why would someone deliberately inflict pain on another being? I just don't understand,' replied Skrinkle, looking rather glum. 'It's my belief that Ballam wanted to rule Veena as well as his own realm. By taking the Diamond Angels from the Lamanya Plinth, he believed he would be able to exert his power over the Veronians. Thankfully for Veena, it didn't quite work out like that. Now that's enough talk for the moment;

we need to make our way to the Hafeena village. Time is ticking on, and there's still so much for you to see.'

Lydia thought how evil Ballam must be. For a moment she feared that she wouldn't be able to help Veena. She was only 12 years old, after all. It didn't make sense to her.

'Little one, what's troubling you?' asked Skrinkle.

'You all believe I can help you, even Lady Ronan did, but what if I can't? What if I am just an ordinary 12-year-old girl who just happens to live in Gwendonia Castle? I'm not special at all; in fact, I can be annoying on occasions. Just ask my brother Ellis. I don't want to let you all down when you realise just how ordinary I really am,' she babbled.

'My dear Lydia, you have inner strength and are stronger than anyone I have ever known. You just need to believe in yourself. You are capable of great, great things. Lady Ronan believed it was your destiny to continue the quest,' said Skrinkle.

'What's my destiny, Skrinkle? To get killed by some evil lunatic and his followers?'' she replied.

'Maybe we are asking too much of you,' Skrinkle smiled sadly. 'When you meet Z later, you will have a tough decision to make, I'm afraid,' he warned her. 'But for now, let's visit the elves.'

Lydia couldn't take in the enormity of what she was being told and felt overwhelmed by everything she had experienced so far: enchanted Veena; meeting the Duons; the Harimau tigers; Uze the Spogly giant; the Tulwen fairies—and now she was on her way to meet elves!

'There are so many twists and turns to this path,' she said.

'I told you,' Laughed Skrinkle.

'There are mushrooms and pumpkins everywhere,' said Lydia excitedly. They were enormous: big enough to sit on. There were lilac mushrooms and blue pumpkins as far as she could see. 'Skrinkle can I sit on one of the mushrooms?' said a delighted Lydia.

'I suppose,' chuckled Skrinkle.

After some difficulty, Lydia managed to climb onto one of the humungous mushrooms.

'It's so soft to sit on,' she exclaimed.

'If you say so,' he laughed.

'I'm coming down,' she yelled, before sliding off the mushroom. She landed awkwardly on the path, her face coming meeting with Skrinkle's paws.

'Enjoyed that, did you?' asked Skrinkle. They both began laughing.

'It was fun,' she giggled.

Skrinkle snapped off a big piece of mushroom and with his paw he shoved the whole lot into his mouth. 'Absolutely delicious,' he said, licking his paws with his tongue.

'You can eat them?'

'Of course, they're a delicacy, perfection. Go on! Try a piece! I'm sure you'll find it yummy,' he enthused.

Lydia snapped a piece off the mushroom and held it between her fingers. 'It won't poison me, will it?'

'Of course not!'

'You have to be careful; back home, we have poisonous mushrooms,' she explained.

'We certainly don't have any mushrooms in Veena that are poisonous. That I can guarantee,' he replied.

Lydia hesitantly put the piece of snapped off mushroom into her mouth and began chewing. 'It tastes like chocolate cake and custard, not like mushroom at all.'

'I don't know what cake and custard is, but by the look on your face it must be delicious,' he giggled.

'Chocolate cake and custard are totally scrumptious Skrinkle! You can try some when we return to Gwendonia if you'd like.'

Lydia ate and ate until she couldn't eat any more.

'I'm stuffed full, Skrinkle,' she sighed, rubbing her stomach.

'That'll teach you! You've eaten too much. You'll never find lilac mushrooms and blue pumpkins anywhere else but here in Veena,' said Skrinkle.'

'Can you eat the pumpkins too?'

'Yes, and they're just as delicious,' he replied.

'I'll try them next time. I can't eat another mouthful, or I'll be sure to vomit.'

'We don't want that, do we? So best not try the pumpkins today,' said Skrinkle. 'Listen, can you hear that sound, Lydia?'

Melodic music could be heard wafting through the trees.

'Where's that coming from?' Lydia asked.

'We are nearing the Hafeena village. The Hafli elves are playing music; they are celebrating,' smiled Skrinkle.

The music was haunting and captivating and she had never heard a melody like it before: she could hear flutes, harps, drums, and a fiddle, and singing.

'What are they celebrating?' she asked inquisitively.

'You, little one! You! They are all eager to meet you,' smiled Skrinkle.

Lydia was in shock. 'They are playing the music for me? That's very kind of them.'

They had reached the end of a cobbled path. Dense vegetation prevented them from going any further, but still they could hear the hauntingly beautiful sound of music.

'How can we get through?' said Lydia impatiently, as she looked up at the trees, bushes, and brambles that blocked their path to the village.

'This is an enchanted world, Lydia. Wonderment is all around you.'

He began rummaging through the inside pocket of his coat and took out a small, gold panpipe. He quickly held it to his mouth and blew into it softly, making the most angelic of melodies. The sound left Lydia feeling rather emotional, and tears welled up in her eyes. Suddenly, the trees, brambles, and bushes slowly began unravelling, making a hole large enough for Skrinkle and Lydia to walk through.

'We can get through, Skrinkle,' said Lydia excitedly.

'Yes, come quickly. The gap will only be open for a few moments, so we need to hurry.'

Skrinkle grabbed Lydia's hand and they ran through the gap. The vegetation began crawling and intertwining, again, leaving no trace of the gap they just run through.

Skrinkle noticed the worry on Lydia's face. 'We can get back, don't worry, Lydia.'

They followed the sound of the music and it grew louder and louder, until there it was: the Hafeena village.

'There must be hundreds of them,' shouted Lydia, staring at great throng of Hafli elves, all playing music, dancing, and singing. Coloured bunting was draped all over their houses and all around the tree branches.

'It's like I've stepped into a fairy-tale book,' smiled Lydia.

'Even in the most wonderful of fairy tales, there is always evil lurking, I'm afraid, Lydia.'

'Oh yes, that hideous Ballam. Just for a moment, I forgot all about him,' replied Lydia.

'Come, let's find Norve. He's the leader of the Hafli elves,' said Skrinkle.

Before Lydia could say another word, a little voice shouted out. 'Skrinkle! Skrinkle! Here, down here.' It was Norve, sitting on the most elaborate wooden throne.

'Ahh, there you are, my friend,' said Skrinkle.

'Please, sit next to me,' said Norve.

Lydia and Skrinkle made their way past the large congregation of elves and sat down on large floral cushions, right in the middle of the village. Lydia studied Norve, who was no more than a few inches in height, with pointy elf ears, a snub nose, and a time-worn face etched with knowledge and wisdom.

'Hello, Lydia. You are just as pretty as Lady Ronan described you,' said Norve.

'Thank you. You knew Lady Ronan?'

'Of course. She remained committed and true to us and cared about every Veronian, throughout her life. We do miss her so,' said Norve.

'I know exactly how you feel. I miss her terribly,' replied Lydia.

'Welcome to Hafeena Lydia! We are so excited that you have made the journey to reach us,' smiled Norve.

'Thank you for letting me visit you. It wasn't the easiest of places to reach,' she said.

'That's how we like it! We don't want to be found by that evil, greedy backstabber! He is the evilest being ever to be created, along with his blasted servants!' Norve's face turning red with anger. *Norve must calm down. I need to take deep breaths*, he said to himself.

'Calm down, Norve, it's no good for you; you'll make yourself unwell,' said Skrinkle.

'I know, you're right. I'll calm down, but I can't forget what he did. He almost destroyed us, didn't he?' said Norve.

'Yes, he did *try*,' replied Skrinkle, looking sombre. 'But didn't quite succeed, did he? Luckily for us, we had the Spogly giants, the Orgara dragons, and the Duons. And let's not forget the Tulwens and every other enchanted being who helped,' added Norve.

'What about you, Norve? And the Haflis? You destroyed hundreds and hundreds of the Sinaras, didn't you?' said Skrinkle.

'Yes, we did. It was the battle of all battles that day.'

Lydia began listening to Norve and Skrinkle talk about all the people who had died in Veena at the hands of the evil and callous Ballam. Who was this person who was causing so much misery? But she knew not to ask Skrinkle any more questions for now. All would be revealed when she met Zavantos.

Norve stood up from his throne and shouted out to the Hafli elves. 'Please, quiet, quiet, quiet! Thank you. I need to address you all.'

You could hear a pin drop, as every elf looked at their leader Norve, Skrinkle, and Lydia.

'My fellow elves, I would like to welcome Lydia to Veena, and to the Hafeena forest. It is a celebratory day, for she will carry on with the quest of the late Lady Ronan,' he continued.

'Don't tell me Skrinkle, Ballam again,' Lydia whispered to Skrinkle.

The elves roared, cheered, and clapped, relieved that Lydia would help them try to defeat Ballam.

'Skrinkle, maybe they may have mistaken me for someone else?' questioned Lydia.

'No, they haven't, Lydia. It's you. They are happy and delighted to see you. This display of affection is for you. We will soon be leaving Hafeena, but for now, we will sit down and enjoy the festivities and celebrations,' smiled Skrinkle.

Lydia addressed the elves. 'I am very honoured, thank you, elves, for your kind and warm welcome.' Lydia didn't fully understand the magnitude of what was going on. However, she thought it polite to thank them for the hospitality being shown to her.

'Thank you too, Norve, it's been wonderful meeting you.'

'Delighted,' Norve replied.

91

While she was saying thank you, she noticed something familiar about Norve's throne. Carved into the wood were cherubs, like those she'd seen at Gwendonia. The throne's seat was made of blue velvet, like the box that contained the Lamanya Stone, and like the inside of the space where she had found the golden key and Diamond Angel amulet.

'Your seat is a lovely colour, Norve,' she said.

'Why, thank you, Lydia. The material is made by the Juga Naiads. They take the saliva from the Bugjub beetle— annoying little creatures and eat everything and who take what is not theirs— which is used to make this gorgeous colour.'

'Juga Naiads, what are they?' Lydia asked.

Norve told her that the Juga Naiads were water goddesses who lived behind the waterfalls in Veena.

'They live in the waterfalls?' asked Lydia eagerly.

'Not *in* the waterfalls, but behind them,' replied Norve. 'But you often see them swimming in the pools below the waterfall.'

'Can I meet them, Skrinkle? Please!' begged Lydia.

'Yes, but not today, I'm afraid. You can definitely meet them when you return,' he assured her. 'Veena is an enormous place, and you are not going to be able to meet everyone today, as you need to return to Gwendonia,' Skrinkle reminded her.

It was time for Lydia and Skrinkle to leave the elves. Lydia reassured them that she would come and visit them the next time she returned to Veena. She'd had the most magical of times, meeting Norve and the Hafli elves. They returned to the edge of the forest, where the Duons were patiently waiting for them. It was time for Lydia to finally meet the great and wise Zavantos.

Chapter 8

The Mighty Zavantos

'Are you ready to meet Zavantos, Lydia?' asked Skrinkle.

'I am, but I'm also a little nervous about what he will tell me, especially about Ballam,' she replied.

Skrinkle and Lydia climbed onto the Duons again, ready to take flight.

'Oh, by the way, you can ask Z as many questions as you wish,' said Skrinkle. 'Let's get going! Ready, 1, 2, 3! Duons, up! Duons, up!' Once again, they were soaring over the picturesque skies of Veena.

'Lydia, look down there,' Skrinkle pointed to some figures bathing in a beautiful pool. It was the water goddesses: the Juga Naiads. Two were swimming in the pool and three were standing by the water's edge, waving at Skrinkle and Lydia as they flew past.

'Are you happy that you've seen them?' laughed Skrinkle.

The Juga Naiads looked like any average human but were exceptionally graceful and captivating.

'I am,' gushed Lydia. 'How far away is Z, Skrinkle? We've been flying for at least 15 minutes.'

'We're nearly there,' he told her. 'There, look Lydia, it's the Lamanya tower, the tower of eternity.' Skrinkle pointed out the tower, which loomed in the distance. Lydia squinted her eyes and could see an enormous white structure as the Duons came into land by a vast body of water. The tower, an imposing structure built out of white marble, stood at the centre of an island in the middle of what was a vast lagoon.

'Who lives there, Skrinkle? Is this where Zavantos is?' asked Lydia.

'Yes, that is where he lives now,' replied Skrinkle.

'But where? I can't see him.' Lydia was scanning all around the island to see Z, but she realised then that she didn't even know what he looked like.

'Oh, don't worry, he is there,' replied Skrinkle.

'We can't swim over to the island. How are we going to get across? Can't the Duons take us? They've taken us everywhere in Veena.'

'I'm afraid not,' said Skrinkle. 'Just watch me.' He stood by the edge of the lake and began calling out. 'Water spirits, please be kind to Lydia and me.'

'What are you doing? What do they do?' said Lydia.

'I'm calling out to the water gods. They guard the Lamanya Tower. We need permission from them to get across the island.'

Skrinkle began calling out three-times. 'Water spirits, let me by so I can reach the other side. The Lamanya Tower I must reach to speak with Zavantos, so he can teach.'

Lydia stood next to Skrinkle, not knowing what was going to happen next. In the water, many ripples appeared, and began moving towards the shore where Lydia and Skrinkle were standing. Two gigantic male water gods rose up from the depths. 'We hear that which you seek, my friend, and we will allow you to cross to the island.'

The two water gods noticed Lydia and looked at Skrinkle for an explanation. 'This is Lydia from the earth plane. She needs to speak with Zavantos.'

'Yes, we are aware of who she is. Welcome to Veena, Lydia.'

'Thank you,' she muttered, while gazing at the gods standing side by side in the water. 'You can see right through them, Skrinkle,' she whispered.

'Yes, well,' they are *water* gods,' Skrinkle explained. They were transparent, but one could still make out the outlines of their faces and torsos.

'Your request has been granted,' one of the gods called out. The other water god whistled a haunting tune, a piercing sound, and Lydia noticed more ripples appearing in the water.

'These will take you across to the island,' one of the male water gods told them, pointing at two giant turtles. 'They will ensure you reach the island safely, where the almighty Zavantos will be waiting for you.'

Lydia observed the turtles, and instantly it made her think of Lady Ronan's exquisite turtle brooch that she always wore.

'Thank you, water gods, for allowing us to cross,' said Skrinkle.

'Yes, thank you very much,' added Lydia, smiling.

'You're both welcome,' they replied, before disappearing beneath the water.

Lydia and Skrinkle walked closer to the edge. 'Jump on!' said Skrinkle, as he stepped effortlessly onto one of the turtle's strong, nacre shell, which shone with an iridescent gleam. Lydia was apprehensive, but she knew that this was the only way she would be able to meet Zavantos. She stepped onto the other turtle's shell and held the reins loosely.

'You'll need a better grip than that! Hold them tightly,' he told her.

She quickly tightened her grip on the reins.

'They go extremely fast. We'll get to the centre of the island in no time.'

'Ready, set, go!' yelled Skrinkle. The turtles flew through the water at speed, with Skrinkle and Lydia holding on to their reins for dear life as water sprayed all over them. They looked at each other and laughed: they were soaking wet again.

'It's like water skiing!' Lydia exclaimed.

'What's that?' said Skrinkle, looking confused.

'I'll tell you later!'

The turtles were nearing the island, and the enormous tower was looming above them. They both stepped off the turtles and onto the island. Skrinkle and Lydia thanked the turtles and waved to them before they disappeared beneath the water.

'This way, Lydia. Zavantos is behind the tower,' said Skrinkle.

'What's he like? Does he look like a Greek god?' Lydia bombarded Skrinkle with questions.

'Greek god? Who, Zavantos? I don't believe so,' Skrinkle chuckled.

Before Lydia could ask another question, there was an almighty roar. 'What's that?' she stammered.

Skrinkle began laughing. 'It's only Z waking up from his nap. He won't harm you!'

'But what is he? He doesn't sound human, or even Veronian,' said Lydia.

'He is very much Veronian, I can assure you. He is the greatest Veronian that has ever lived,' replied Skrinkle.

When they had walked behind the Lamanya tower, Lydia gasped. 'Z-Z-Zavantos is a dragon? A real-life dragon?'

Zavanthos rose up above them, flapping his almighty wings, his red and green scaly skin glinting, along with his piercing green eyes and huge teeth that could kill instantly with one bite. Fireballs burst from his huge nostrils, which made the ground beneath him sizzle. His claws were gigantic and as sharp and deadly as his teeth. One swipe of Zavantos' claws would ensure a quick death.

Skrinkle noticed Lydia's fear. 'He is the loveliest of dragons you could ever wish to meet. But don't be fooled by his friendliness. After all, he is a dragon, and will protect Veena at all costs. He is the leader and the noblest of the Ogara dragons; in fact, he's the bravest dragon that has ever lived.'

Skrinkle and Lydia approached Zavantos. 'Ah, Skrinkle, my dear friend—and Lydia, sweet Lydia. I am so pleased to finally meet you. I've heard so many wonderful about you,' said Zavantos.

'Thank you, Zavantos. That is so kind of you to say. I am so pleased to be finally meeting you too,' replied Lydia, smiling.

'Lydia, may I introduce to you the mighty Zavantos, leader of the Ogara dragons and protector of Veena,' said Skrinkle, looking immensely proud and honoured to be in the dragon's presence.

'Thank you, my dear friend, for the lovely introduction,' Zavantos said, chuckling. His head was tilted back, revealing his enormous teeth.

'May I ask you, Zavantos, what wonderful things have you heard about me?' asked Lydia.

'Oh Lydia, Lydia, where do I start? I know you are devoted to your family and love them and Gwendonia more than anything else in the world. I know that you have the purest and kindest of hearts, and that you are kind to others and will go out of your way to help anyone who needs it,' replied Zavantos. 'Lovely qualities wouldn't you say?'

'Thank you very much, but I'm not always kind to my brother. We do argue and get on one another's nerves,' she replied nervously.

'Yes, I know you do, but let me tell you, all siblings argue, Lydia. I know that you love each other, and that's the most important thing,' he smiled. 'Have you liked Veena so far?'

'I have loved every minute! I would love to return at some point. Would that be, OK?' she asked enthusiastically.

'Of course! Think of Veena as your home, but you must never tell anyone of our existence, Lydia: this is very important. Do you understand?' said Zavantos.

'Yes, I understand. Totally,' she reassured him.

'Please sit beside me, Lydia, and you, my dear friend Skrinkle,' said Zavantos.

Skrinkle and Lydia managed to find a small patch of green grass next to Z, which he had not as yet managed to set on fire and sat next to him. Lydia was waiting in anticipation for Zavantos to tell her all about Veena and, of course, the sinister Ballam.

Zavantos walked around in a circle several times before sitting down on his back legs, his enormous wings tucked in by his sides, and exhaled loudly. 'Lydia, I am going to tell you all about the annals of Veena.'

'What are annals?' asked Lydia.

'Annals are a chronological record of events that have taken place. I'm going to tell you about everything that has happened here, including the near-destruction of Veena at the hands of the evil Ballam. Now, let's begin. I know you have many questions, and I thank you for being patient with Skrinkle, for it is I who must tell you about Veena. I sent Skrinkle to protect you and keep you safe. Lady Ronan and I believed that you were the one to help us. As you are aware, Lydia, there is always good and evil. I know that on your earth plane good has to fight evil too.'

Lydia did not understand wars and battles. What was the point? War just brought pain and suffering to others. 'This place is extraordinary and seems peaceful. Why do you have an army and battles?' she asked.

'Sadly, all is not what it appears, Lydia,' Zavantos told her.

'Veena was created by celestial beings called Ezra, Seraphina, and Celeste. Alongside Veena, they created the realm of Taros, to the north. For many centuries there was peace between the two realms, with no concerns. Both realms grew in prosperity, with everyone living harmoniously. In Veena, we are known as the Veronians. Taros people are known as the Tarosas. I know that you haven't been to the Veronian village yet, but you will meet them when you return to Veena, I promise,'' he said.

'Thank you, Zavantos,' replied Lydia. 'There wasn't enough time to meet everyone,' she added.

'The Veronians are eager to meet you, and I know that they'll be a little envious that you had the opportunity to meet the Tulwens and Haflis. And Uze—a very hardworking giant indeed,' smiled Zavantos.

'He's great, but he has terrible hay fever. He snotted all over us, didn't he, Lydia? And the Duons. Piles and oodles of snot everywhere. Disgusting!' shuddered Skrinkle.

Skrinkle and Lydia giggled as they remembered their encounter with Uze. Zavantos joined in the laughter.

'How are the Spoglys?' asked Zavantos.

'They are well, I believe, but we only saw Uze. He was busy making his weapons. The others were high in mountains and deep in the forests. They feel that there is unrest coming to Veena,' said Skrinkle, looking tense.

'The truth is we don't know if or when Ballam will return. But what we do know is that we must be prepared for all eventualities,' said Zavantos. So,' let me return to my story.'

'When the rulers of Taros disappeared, their son Ballam became ruler. He was, let's just say, a very different ruler to his parents. He was envious that Veena had been created before Taros and equally envious of the sacred Lamanya Plinth, which held the Diamond Angels. There was such evil coursing through his veins,' continued Zavantos.

Zavantos pointed a claw towards the Lamanya Tower. 'Come, let me show you the Lamanya plinth.'

Lydia and Skrinkle followed Zavantos towards the entrance of the tower. His colossal tail gently swayed with every step that he took, and his mighty claws dug into the ground beneath him, leaving gigantic footprints in the brown soil. The three of them made their way through the enormous marble door. There stood the plinth, guarded by life-size marble statues.

Lydia noticed that Tulwen fairies, Hafli elves, Ogara dragons, Duon dragonflies, and Spogly giants were carved into the marble. It was an impressive piece of work.

'The plinth depicts the annals of Veena. The marble frieze takes you on a journey from the beginning up until that terrible night where Ballam tried to destroy us,' explained Zavantos.

Studying the frieze, she could see the battle taking place between the Veronians and the Tarosas. And there he was: Ballam, with a skeletal face and large wings, standing among his army, frozen in time in the marble frieze.

Lydia had a flashback to her nightmare. There was something eerily similar about this Ballam, surrounded by his army. Lydia couldn't move and continued to stare at the frieze. 'Are you OK, Lydia?' asked Zavantos, concerned.

Lydia told Zavantos and Skrinkle about the nightmare that she'd had the night before Lady Ronan died.

'I was petrified. I feel it was more of a premonition now I know the secrets of Gwendonia and that this evil being is real.'

'Wherever he is on the earth plane, it seems inevitable that I'll meet him,' she said sombrely.

'You all looked so joyful up until that terrible night,' said Lydia.

'We were the happiest,' replied Skrinkle and Zavantos.

'Let me tell you about the sacred plinth and the reason we need your help. The Lamanya Plinth, as you can see, is tall and made from solid marble. At the top you can see a large glass dome with three golden branches inside. Do you notice anything?' asked Zavantos.

'I can see the golden branches,' said Lydia.

'Look closer, at the ends of each branch,' he prompted.

Lydia peered up at the branches. At the tip of each was a sort of platform, in the shape of an angel. 'Oh yes, I can see angel shapes.'

'That's right, Lydia, but notice that they are empty,' said Zavantos, pointing with a claw.

'What's missing?' she asked, puzzled.

'The plinth held three diamond-shaped angels,' he replied. 'One for Ezra, one for Seraphina, and one for Celeste: one for each celestial being.'

Lydia thought for a moment. 'I think I have one of them!' Hurriedly, she rummaged in her bag and fished out the diamond-shaped angel.

Zavantos and Skrinkle smiled. 'Yes, we knew that you had one of them,' said Zavantos.

'When I ventured to the round tower in the middle of the night, I found it in Lady Ronan's bedroom, after the Harimau tigers helped me. It was hidden away in the wood carving.'

'You, my dear Lydia, were meant to find the Diamond Angel, the golden key and, of course, my old and dearest friend Skrinkle. And you have taken good care of them all. You had to find the angel yourself, with no help from Skrinkle,' Zavantos told her.

'But why not? I thought I was going mad, hearing noises and seeing things move,' said Lydia.

'Skrinkle wasn't able to intervene. It was only when you had found the door to our world he was able to speak to you,' Zavantos continued.

'He did frighten me in the tunnel when he started talking,' Lydia chuckled.

'I can imagine he did startle you,' said Zavantos, smiling at Skrinkle. 'On the night of the battle, Ballam and his servants, the Sinaras, invaded Veena and attempted to taking the three Diamond Angels from the golden branches. Ballam thought that taking the Diamond Angels from the sacred plinth would increase his power over both Taros and Veena and allow him to create new realms.

'New realms?' asked Lydia.

'The Diamond Angels are powerful. Together, the three of them created the ultimate Aeon…Veena,' he smiled.

Aeon? what does that mean asked Lydia.

'It means power of eternity'.

'What Ballam didn't realise was that the prophecy incited by the celestial beings warned that anyone who purposely took the Diamond Angels to gain power and inflict injury and death to all Veronians would be banished to another world,' sighed Zavantos.

100

Lydia listened carefully, trying to take in the enormity of what he was telling her.

'Ballam crossed the lake onto the island and entered the Lamanya Tower, making his way to the scared plinth. The water gods weren't guarding the island, as we had believed there wasn't any need. He took out the diamond-shaped angels one by one. When the first Diamond Angel was disturbed, there was an almighty noise, and rocks from the mountains came crashing down. His servants, the Sinaras, killed anyone who tried to stop him. Unfortunately, we were unprepared for battle,' said Zavantos, shaking his head. 'He took the second then the third. It was catastrophic. We felt the whole ground shaking violently, and the mountains erupting and moving. Until finally, Veena was split into three spheres.

'W…What?' Lydia gasped.

'Yes, Veena has been separated. Ballam didn't get to keep the Diamond Angels; one was found in the foundations of Gwendonia, along with the golden key—the one you must use to enter the golden doorway between our worlds. There is only one golden key, and it opens all three doorways between the three spheres. We haven't been able to find the remaining two doorways.'

'So, they're like portals to another dimension?' she asked.

'Yes,' replied Skrinkle.

'You see, Lydia, Ballam believed that he could enslave us. Instead, Ballam, along with his servants, was banished to the earth plane.'

'What do you mean? He lives on earth? But why earth? You could have banished him somewhere else, not to where I live,' replied Lydia.

'On earth, his powers are limited and much weaker, Lydia. He can't return to Veena or Taros unless he finds the doorway between our worlds. One which happens to be in the foundations of Gwendonia. This is the reason I need to protect it night and day, for fear that someday he'll return,' said Zavantos.

'We know what Ballam looks like from the frieze,' said Lydia.

101

'Ballam along with the Sinarars are also known as Odium Morphs—they can change appearance. They follow the dark Zagan,' said Zavantos.

'Hang on, what is the dark Zagan? asked Lydia.

'The practice of the dark arts. Simply put- pure evil,' he replied. 'Would you continue in the quest? I won't pretend that it's not going to be dangerous, Lydia. He will not care if you are a young girl. That's why I sent Skrinkle, to guide and protect you'.

'How exactly do you want me to help you?' asked Lydia.

'Why, to continue to look for the two diamond angels, which will hopefully lead you to the two remaining doorways of Veena. It is only when *all* three diamond angels are placed back into the golden branches within the scared Lamanya plinth Veena can become one again. And only then will Ballam and his servants be destroyed', said Zavantos.

'It'll be like trying to find a needle in a haystack! Almost impossible to find without any clues. So, let's be clear Ballam and his servants are on earth? You need me to continue the quest to find the missing two diamond angels? and I have Skrinkle to protect me?' sighed Lydia.

'Lady Ronan adored and believed in you. She left Gwendonia to you because she knew how much you loved it, and that you would never sell it to anyone, thereby keeping the doorway between your world and ours safe,' Zavantos explained.

'You're right, Zavantos, I would never sell Gwendonia, never,' said Lydia, her eyes filling with tears.

'She adored Veena and throughout her life would visit often. We miss her so,' said Zavantos.

'The Harimau tigers, the Asiras and Woodilfs, who reside at the castle, will also endeavour to keep you safe,' continued Zavantos.

'What if I'm not at the castle? Who will try and keep me safe, apart from Skrinkle?' questioned Lydia.

'Never worry, sweet Lydia. There's enchantment all around you, no matter where you go on the earth plane,' replied Zavantos. 'If you feel that you are not able to help us, Lydia, we completely understand. But you will need to destroy the golden key as soon as you return home. As you know' it's the only key that will open all three doors to Veena.

'I understand.'

Lydia looked at Skrinkle and noticed his eyes were teary. 'What's wrong, Skrinkle?'

'If you can't help us, I'll have to leave you, little one, once we reach Gwendonia. Once the key is destroyed, the doorway will be closed for all eternity.'

'So, if I decide not to help you and the key is destroyed, Veena will forever be divided, and I'll never see you again?' she asked.

'That's correct, and Ballam and the Sinaras will wander earth, plotting and trying to find a way to return. It would be disastrous,' Zavantos told Lydia.

'Who lives in Taros now?' she asked.

'As far as we know, no one lives there now. It's deserted, and we have never ventured there since that fateful night,' Zavantos told her.

'I just have to help you. I can't destroy the golden key, knowing that I could have helped you, and that your world is in the foundations of Gwendonia. I will spend my entire life trying to help you, although I can't promise that I'll be able to find the other two missing Diamond Angels and doorways. But I'll try my hardest,' she continued.

Zavantos and Skrinkle looked at each other. 'Lady Ronan would be proud of you; she was brave like you,' said Zavantos.

'I don't feel very brave,' she admitted, looking down at her feet.

'Lydia, you are very brave. Every Veronian will be forever grateful to you for continuing on the quest,' said Zavantos.

'But I'm going to Ireland, and then New York, visiting family, and I'll be away from Gwendonia for three weeks,' she panicked. 'I won't be able to help or visit you.'

'Don't you worry, Veena has been divided for many, many, many years,' replied Zavantos, while patting her shoulder.

'Lydia, enjoy every moment with your family; it's important to always be there for one another,' said Zavantos, while walking out of the Lamanya Tower.

Lydia noticed the sadness in Zavantos' face. 'What's wrong with him, Skrinkle?'

'We all have family that we haven't seen for many, many years.'

Lydia shook her head in disbelief: she could not comprehend the evilness of Ballam.

Lydia walked up to Zavantos, who was wiping a tear away from his eye with his ginormous claw. 'Everything will be OK, I promise,' she reassured him. 'You miss your family terribly, don't you?'

'Yes, I do, sweet Lydia. Not a day goes by without me not thinking of them,' he replied.

'Aren't you lonely on your own here on the island?' she asked.

'I'm never on my own Lydia, I have my memories of happy times with my family. But I do have many visitors: the Tulwens, the Haflis . . . Oh look, here comes Pilly now.' He pointed towards the sky.

'Who's Pilly?' asked Lydia, as the creature flew nearer to them before gracefully landing next to Zavantos. Pilly was an exceptionally tall and elegant yellow butterfly, and had the daintiest of faces and huge, colourful wings.

'Welcome Pilly, I haven't seen you for a while—what have you been doing?' Zavantos asked.

'Hello, Zavantos, Skrinkle and, of course you, Miss Lydia! Welcome to Veena,' said Pilly. 'I don't think you are going to like what I'm about to tell you,' Zavantos.

'Pilly, what have you done now?'

Pilly was a curious and adventurous butterfly, but her curiosity often put her in danger. 'You know there is unrest in Veena, like something is about to happen? You know what I'm talking about: even the Spoglys sense it. They are in the mountains and forests to make sure that we are all safe,' she said.

'Go on, Pilly, tell me what's happened,' commanded Zavantos.

'One night I was at Tulwen castle, and Tint and I were talking about, *you-know-who*.'

'Yes,' I know who you are referring to,' replied Zavantos.

'Afterwards, I had this urge to fly to Taros to see if Ballam or his servants had returned,' Pilly said, hanging her head in shame.

'What were you thinking? You put yourself in danger, venturing into Taros,' said Zavantos angrily.

'I know I did, and I won't ever go there again. I wanted to see if Ballam, has an army waiting to attack Veena,' she replied, her eyes filled with tears.

'Anything could have happened to you,' said Skrinkle.

'I was wrong to even go there, but I suppose I was prepared to die for Veena. I feel he is getting stronger the longer he's on earth. I believe he is mastering his powers, and it is only a matter of time before his return,' she trembled.

'Pilly, what did you see in Taros?' asked Lydia eagerly.

'When I flew across the border, I saw no sign of life. The place looked deserted, or so I thought. Taros is dark, even in the daytime. I flew for miles until I reached Taros Castle. I knew I shouldn't have, but I went inside and began looking around for any clue or sign of life, but I saw nothing. It was quiet, eerily quiet, in the castle. Then I reached the great hall,' she wailed.

'What did you see in the great hall?' demanded Zavantos.

'It's too awful to say,' she cried.

'Tell me Pilly,' he continued.

I, I, saw several Spogly and Ogara heads mounted on the wall, and a roaring fire was burning. It was cold, freezing. You'd never think it was summer; it felt more like winter there. The lit fire meant someone was at the castle. I was so scared. I flew and flew and didn't stop flying until I reached Veena. What if some of the Sinaras are still there? What if not all of them left when they were banished to earth?' she cried.

Pilly didn't dare tell Zavantos that she had flown to Taros on several occasions, but she had never ventured to Taros castle until that last time.

'Something is going on in Taros. I can't say for certain that there are no Sinaras there, but I can assure you Ballam remains on earth, that I can guarantee,' said Zavantos.

'But who could be at the castle? I thought they were all banished,' said Skrinkle.

'Yes, me too, which is why we always need to be on our guard at all times. I'm afraid, my dear friend. The truth is, we don't know how many Veronians Ballam and the Sinaras killed,' said Zavantos.

Lydia's eyes welled with tears as she thought about the severed heads mounted on the wall at Taros Castle. Were they members of Uze's and Zavantos' families? Probably. And their heads were being displayed as trophies for the pleasure of this callous and evil monster, Ballam, no doubt. It was too gruesome to comprehend, which made Lydia feel fearful of what Ballam and the Sinaras were capable of.

'You must promise me, Pilly, that you will never do anything like that again, do you understand? Do not leave Veena,' ordered Zavantos. 'You are lucky that the Spellters never caught you or you'd be in serious, serious trouble with Professor Quelldar.'

'I know I would be in deep trouble, and as punishment, I'd have to work with that Lutin,' she scowled.

'Exactly! And you wouldn't want that, would you?' said Zavantos, while Pilly shook her head in disagreement.

'What are Spellters? Are there many of them?' asked Lydia.

'The Spellters are masters of magic, and they live in Wardis House, which is between the mountains and forest. They will alert the Veronians should we be attacked by Taros,' said Zavantos. 'There are four of them, including Professor Dorivor Quelldar.'

'I'd like to meet them,' said Lydia.

'And you shall,' smiled Zavantos. 'I would take you myself, but I can't ever leave the island, Lydia. I must protect the sacred Lamanya Plinth.'

'I don't want to leave you, Zavantos,' said Lydia.

'Sweet Lydia, I'll be here when you return. I'm not going anywhere. You sound just like Lady Ronan,' he smiled. Lydia threw her arms around his gigantic neck and kissed him on the top of his nose.

'OK, I'll see you soon, I promise. Goodbye, Pilly, it was lovely meeting you,' beamed Lydia.

'Goodbye, Lydia,' replied Pilly.

'Skrinkle, please look after Lydia. She will need to quickly meet the Spellters before you leave. She'll need the discs before returning to earth,' Zavantos told him.

'I will look after her with my life, dear friend, and I'll take her to the Spellters before we return to Gwendonia.'

Zavantos and Pilly watched as Lydia and Skrinkle climbed back onto the turtles once more to cross the lake and to where the Duons were once again patiently waiting.

Back on the shore, Lydia stepped off her turtle and waved enthusiastically to Zavantos and Pilly, who were still watching from the island.

'Isn't he magnificent, Lydia?' said Skrinkle.

'Yes, he is. I can't wait to visit him again,' she replied, becoming emotional. 'Zavantos is such a wise dragon. It's heartbreaking that he always has to guard the Lamanya Plinth because of what's happened here,' she said.

'It is. Now you know why it is so difficult to even reach the island, and why we needed permission from the water gods,' said Skrinkle.

'Yes, I understand now.'

Skrinkle and Lydia climbed onto the Duons and took to the skies once again.

'We don't have much time, but we will quickly visit the Spellters,' Skrinkle shouted.

'Yes!' Lydia shrieked excitedly.

'I knew you would say that,' laughed Skrinkle. Soon they found themselves standing outside Wardis House, the home of the Spellters.

'Lydia, we don't have much time and Professor Quelldar, he's very friendly and . . . talkative. What I'm saying is, we can't say here long as we need to return to Gwendonia.'

'OK, Skrinkle, I understand.'

They approached Wardis House and stood outside the door. Before Skrinkle could pick up the doorknob, the door quietly opened on its own.

'Come in,' come in. Don't be standing at the door,' called out a friendly male voice.

Lydia looked at Skrinkle, excitedly.

'It's the Professor, Lydia,' Skrinkle laughed.

The Professor greeted Skrinkle and Lydia with a bright smile. 'Professor Quelldar, this is Lydia,' said Skrinkle.

'I know all about you, Lydia,' the Professor smiled. He was elderly in appearance, with a trimmed grey beard, and thick, short, wavy grey hair. He was dressed smartly in black trousers, white shirt and black shoes, and wore gold-coloured spectacles. The one item of clothing that made the Professor stand out was his burgundy-coloured waistcoat, with round golden buttons, and a matching cravat, made from the same velvet material.

Professor Quelldar looked nothing like Lydia had expected. She had imagined someone in a floor-length patterned cloak and pointy hat, just like the illustrations in her numerous fairy-tale books.

'It's a pleasure to meet you, Professor,' said Lydia.

'Welcome to Wardis, Lydia, and more importantly, Veena,' he said.

Skrinkle and Lydia walked into the potion room, where the Professor rummaged around at his wooden table, crammed with lots of clay pots containing different ingredients. There were also lots of glass tubes containing various coloured liquids, and two large, black, iron cauldrons full of something luminous that was gently bubbling away. It smelt like sulphur.

'I'll be with you shortly. I just need to throw these last few ingredients into the pot, and I'll be all yours,' he said with a wicked chuckle.

Skrinkle and Lydia heard the Professor reading the ingredients to himself from a large book.

Quelldar's Potion #22
1.   One drop of blood from the Bubjub beetle
2.   One drop of blood from the Ridib Bird
3.   A few toenail clippings from the Mighty Zavantos
4.   Three ladles of the Spogly giant's snot
5.   A pinch of parsley

'Oh, actually, I might leave out the last ingredient: there'll be no parsley in this potion,' he muttered, while chuckling. He began to scoop out giant's snot from a large wooden barrel. Lydia began to feel queasy and remembered how Uze had snotted all over her and Skrinkle.

'I know what happened to you both,' said the Professor, and shook his head. 'Uze snotted all over you, didn't he? I've told him to take his tablets, but will he listen? No, he most certainly won't.'

The Professor pointed to a stack of large, white round discs. The discs were as big as dustbin lids and were neatly piled up by the front door. 'See there? Uze's hay fever tablets. I made them two weeks ago, and he hasn't even bothered to collect them. No wonder he is snotting absolutely everywhere,' the Professor sighed.

Although the Professor was a little eccentric, Lydia found him warm, humorous, and, at times, absent-minded.

'How have you been, Professor?' asked Skrinkle.

'Fine, Skrinkle, thank you. You see this potion? I'm making it for the cinder darts. It's a deadly potion,' he explained.

The Professor started to add other ingredients into his potion. 'One pinch of moss from the Haveena Forest, one large lump of dung from the Duons . . . yes, that should do it!' he shouted, clasping his hands in delight.

'The potion does smell, Professor,' said Lydia, while pinching her nose with her fingers to stop her from inhaling the putrid smell.

'Yes, it's a rancid smell all right, I agree, but it's the best potion to kill that malevolent Ballam and his servants, should they ever return!' he yelled out, his face turning red. 'Sorry, sorry for my outburst, but you know how I get, Skrinkle. I cannot bear the thought of that sinister being.'

'Zavantos told me all about Ballam, Professor: he sounds truly evil,' said Lydia.

'We'll be ready for him, should he ever return, Lydia,' replied the Professor.

Lydia's eyes wandered over the long wooden table. Next to the cauldrons she saw an old, heavy-looking, leather-bound book with gold lettering in italics on the front cover. It was an inscription identical to the inscription she'd seen in the diamond-shaped angel. She began building up the words in her head, as she didn't understand what they meant.

'Anti . . .kva . . .Lekt . . .var,' she repeated. 'Excuse me, Professor, what does *Antikva Lektvar* mean?'

The Professor chuckled. 'It means the ancient book of potions, and it's been here since Veena was created. Let me tell you, there are more than 100,000 potion recipes in this book, including those for curing an upset stomach, from eating too many mushrooms. I know you've tried them – delicious, aren't they?' The Professor winked at her and giggled.

Lydia was speechless that the Professor knew that she had eaten too much of the mushroom on her way to meet the Hafli elves.

'Oh, you saw me, did you?' said Lydia sheepishly.

'Yes,' laughed the Professor. 'As I was saying, the potions can cure upset tummies and even hay fever. I'm an outstanding professor, I have to admit,' he beamed, his chest puffed up with pride. 'Within the pages of this ancient book, you'll find recipes for deadliest potions. You know what he has done to us Lydia, and we must never be complacent; we must always be prepared for his return. You too must always keep your wits about you, when you return to earth. He's clever, cunning, and charming, but he will kill you without a second thought if he realises you know the truth. I don't want to frighten you. I am just warning you to keep yourself safe, Lydia.'

'I know how dangerous the quest is, Professor,' replied Lydia.

'You have me to look after you too, Lydia,' replied Skrinkle.

'Wardis House is very quiet, Professor—no apprentices?'

'Lutin and the others are due back soon; they have gone into the forest to collect plants and herbs to make the potions,' he replied.

'Who is Lutin?' asked Lydia, remembering that Zavantos and Pilly had mentioned his name earlier.

'Lutin . . . Lutin . . . where do I begin? Well, he's my servant,'' chuckled the Professor. 'He's been with me forever. He is loyal but can be extremely frustrating at times.'

'He's a funny little character, is Lutin,' Skrinkle whispered into Lydia's ear.

'I am eager to meet him,' she replied excitedly.

'He has an unusual personality, let's put it like that,' smiled Skrinkle.

'Unusual personality! Oh, I do like how you've described Lutin, Skrinkle. Unusual personality,' chuckled the Professor, shaking his head. 'Wait until I tell him.'

Suddenly, the front door flew open and in stomped a three-foot, funny-looking character.

'Ah, Lutin, you're back,' said the Professor.

'That's Lutin?' asked Lydia, with her mouth open.

'The one and only,' laughed Skrinkle.

Lutin was not what Lydia had expected at all. His face looked aged and grumpy; he had very short-cropped, dark-brown hair, large ears that poked out, a round nose, and a potbelly. He was wearing brown boots, which were mud-caked and worn. He wore a short, bottle-green tabard that stopped just above his knobbly knees.

'Me not happy, master. Lutin not happy with Yogan and Hansa,' he huffed.

'Why? What have they done to you, Lutin?' the Professor questioned.

'Me don't want to talk about it, thank you very much indeed,' he replied, scowling.

'If you don't tell me what they've done to you, then how can I help you?' said the Professor.

'They both threw me in a bucket and lowered me down the water well, a deep well that went down and down. Me was so scared, master,' said Lutin, who was feeling very sorry for himself.

'Yogan and Hansa wouldn't have sent you down the well for fun. They must have wanted something from inside the well, Lutin. Now stop being so dramatic,' said the Professor, pointing at Lutin.

'They wanted me to collect the plants that grow deep in the crevices of the walls,' he scowled.

'Exactly, so they didn't throw you down the water well, did they? It's because you're so small—'.

Lutin looked blankly at the Professor with his head tilted to the side, waiting.

'—I mean, because of your size. You can fit into the bucket, Lutin. You know that you were the best person to collect the delicate floren plants, as these are required for the potions. Now stop making out that they have been unkind to you,' said the Professor sternly.

Lutin stood with his arms folded and with the deepest of frowns etched on his face.

'Hello, Lutin,' said Skrinkle, waving his paw.

111

Lutin hadn't noticed Skrinkle or Lydia, as he was too busy trying to get both Yogan and Hansa into trouble with the Professor.

'Hello, Skrinkle,' Lutin replied, 'and who's that with you?' He pointed at Lydia.

'I'm Lydia, and it's nice to meet you, Lutin,' she said.

'*The* Lydia? The one who's helping us?' he asked.

'Yes, I guess I am the one,' she replied.

'Try and be nice, Lutin,' begged the Professor.

'Lutin always lovely. What are you talking about? Lutin is the loveliest and most obedient of all servants,' he replied.

'Where are Yogan and Hansa, Lutin?' asked the Professor.

'Um, I don't really know. They shouldn't be too long,' he replied, looking mischievous.

'You had better not have done anything to them, Lutin, I mean it. Don't you dare go wandering off,' warned the Professor.

'I 'ain't wandering off, great master,' he mumbled under his breath. 'Me can't have minutes to myself. It's always Lutin, Lutin, Lutin. That's all me hear.'

'I hear quite a sarcastic tone there, Lutin,' the Professor smirked.

'I don't be sarcastic, master. I don't know what that word mean,' he replied.

'Oh yes you do. You know perfectly well what that word means, Lutin,' the Professor said sternly. Lutin had the biggest smile on his face as he walked out of the room.

'Where is he going, Skrinkle?' asked Lydia.

'Who knows, but he'll be in trouble when Yogan and Hansa return. I can feel it.'

'You're right Skrinkle, Lutin does have an unusual personality,' she giggled.

The Professor was waiting outside the front door, waiting for his apprentices to return.

'They're coming,' Lydia. I can hear their voices,' said Skrinkle.

'There you are. Where have you two been?' shouted the Professor.

Skrinkle could hear Yogan and Hansa talking to the Professor, and, by their tone, they sounded very unhappy. The pair walked into the house with the Professor, raging.

'Lutin! Get here at once!' yelled Yogan.

'You'd better come in this room now. You don't want us to come looking for you,' shouted Hansa, as Skrinkle and Lydia watched.

The Professor introduced Lydia to Yogan and Hansa, and they welcomed her to Wardis House. Yogan and Hansa were brothers and apprentices of Professor Quelldar. Yogan looked about the same age as Ellis, Lydia's brother. He was tall, with shoulder-length black hair and light-blue eyes. Hansa looked a few years older than Yogan, and had neck-length, dark-brown hair and piercing green eyes.

'We are sorry that we were preoccupied when we first came in and began yelling for Lutin,' Hansa explained.

'Not to worry. Lutin's been up to his old tricks again, has he?' asked Skrinkle.

'I'm afraid he has, Skrinkle,' said Yogan.

'Lutin! Lutin! Come here at once!' the Professor cried.

'Me coming! No need to be screaming, is there?' he shouted back. In walked Lutin. 'What have me done? Me haven't done anything. Lutin is good.'

'Good? You must be joking,' replied Yogan. 'You lost all the Floren plants. You emptied the bucket of plants down the water well. You threw clumps of moss and muck at us. You set the Ridib bird on us, and we fell and ended stuck in a deep crevice in the mountains!' he yelled.

'You got out, didn't you? How did you get out, by the way?' asked Lutin with a slight smirk.

'You did all those things to Yogan and Hansa?' asked the Professor angrily.

'No, they do not tell the true story, master.'

'Will you stop lying at once,' said Yogan. 'I am never going into the forest or mountains with you again, Lutin. Do you understand?'

'Lutin, go to your room until I decide what the consequences are for your actions,' said the Professor. Lutin shuffled off with his head down. Once he had gone, the Professor asked Yogan and Hansa how they had managed to get out of the deep crevice.

'The Spoglys were in the mountains, and they heard us calling for help. They came and got us out,' replied Hansa.

'Good old Spoglys. Oh well, I'll make Lutin pay for what he has done,' said the Professor distractedly, as he began looking frantically around the room. 'I can't find them, where are they? Where did I put them?'

'What are you looking for, Professor?' asked Yogan.

'My spectacles, I've looked everywhere. I can't seem to find them. You better not have taken them again, Lutin!' he shouted.

Lydia and Skrinkle helped in the search for the Professor's spectacles. Lydia looked up at the spiral staircase, which led onto a large mezzanine, where there were shelves full of books, and spotted Lutin sitting there, legs crossed, with the Professor's gold spectacles on the tip of his nose, reading a book. Lutin knew that Lydia had spotted him, and he pressed his finger to his mouth as if to tell her to be quiet.

'Please go and find Lutin, Yogan. I need my spectacles to complete my potions,' said the flustered Professor. Before Yogan could leave, Lutin suddenly leapt off the shelf, flew down the staircase, and pretended that he had found the Professor's spectacles.

'Here be your spectacles, master. Lutin found them. I should have a reward now, shouldn't I?' said Lutin, looking proud.

'My dear Lutin, most faithful and obedient servant . . . Reward? You pinched them again, didn't you? And you expect a reward?' the Professor raged.

'No, Lutin don't need a reward master. Me thanking you very much,' said Lutin, as he ran towards the door. Skrinkle and Lydia began giggling as Lutin had been caught out.

'Actually, Lutin, I have just the reward for you for pretending to find my spectacles and for setting the Ridib bird on Yogan and Hansa. You can go and feed the groylers!' he said with a wicked grin.

'No! Anything but that! Lutin don't want to feed the groylers, master. They can be vicious.' Lutin looked petrified.

'They are only vicious towards you, Lutin, because you eat their food. Now go. They need to be fed,' said the Professor emphatically.

'Groylers? What are they?' asked Lydia.

'They look like little monsters, with funny little faces and with wings on their backs. They patrol the border between Veena and Taros,' said Skrinkle.

'Can I see them?' asked Lydia.

'Of course,' said the Professor. 'Go with Yogan. He will look after you while Skrinkle and I have a long-awaited catch-up.'

'This way, Lydia,' said Yogan, showing her to the door.

He led Lydia to a large barn next to Wardis House. Yogan opened the barn door and there was Lutin, trying to feed the groylers.

'Get back! Get back! I'm trying to feed you! You're nothing but pests, the lot of you!' Lutin squawked. One of the groylers picked up Lutin with a claw and threw him into a water barrel, leaving him soaked. All the other groylers laughed, their high-pitched screeching was so loud that Lydia had to cover ears with her hands.

'That's enough,' Yogan cried, while tapping the groylers' heads affectionately.

'Lutin, get out of the barrel.'

'No, I'm not. I'm safer in here!' he whined.

'You can't stay in there. You need to get out.' Yogan pulled Lutin out of the water barrel. 'Go and change your wet clothes. I'll feed the groylers.'

Dripping wet, Lutin waved his fists at the groylers. 'I'm never feeding you again, never! Or checking on you, you're a nasty bunch! I don't care what the master says. You're an evil lot. You hate Lutin, and Lutin ain't fussy on you lot neither. I hope you starve,' he shrieked.

'Go, Lutin. You're making things worse,' said Yogan.

'Worse? I was thrown in a barrel of water and nearly drowned by that lot.' Lutin spluttered then pretended to cough.

'There's nothing wrong with you. The water was only up to your neck! Drowned? You are so dramatic, Lutin,' said Yogan.

Lutin scowled and left the barn.

'Is he always like this?' asked Lydia.

'He can be nice when he wants to be, but he does have his moments, as you've seen for yourself today,' smiled Yogan.

Yogan began feeding the groylers, and they appeared to like him. They were affectionate towards him and began nudging his hands with their noses, as if inviting him to stroke them.

'They like you, Yogan,' said Lydia.

'They're great. I never had any problems with them,' he said.

'They look like gargoyles,' said Lydia, as Yogan stroked one particularly persistent groyler.

Yogan looked slightly confused. 'What are gargoyles?'

'You find them on castle walls and in books. They are sentry figures who protect buildings from evil. In my world they do, anyway,' she explained.

'They do sound similar. That's what the groylers are doing: protecting Veena from evil,' said Yogan. 'What's it like where you live?' he asked.

'I live in a castle called Gwendonia. I thought I was losing my mind. A lot of strange events were taking place I couldn't quite understand. I never thought I would find a doorway between our two worlds in the castle's foundations.'

' I am glad it's there,' smiled Yogan.

Lydia told Yogan all about her family, the cove, the pond, and that she would be visiting her grandparents in a place called Ireland. As she was telling Yogan about her life, she remembered that she needed to return to Gwendonia. 'I've got to go. I've got to get back to home,' she panicked.

'Can't you stay a little longer?' Yogan asked.

'I would love to stay, but my family will be leaving for Ireland in a few hours and if my family has to look for me . . . I'll be in big trouble,' she told him.

'Please come back to Veena, Lydia. You will, won't you?'

'I will. I promise I'll come back in a few weeks,' she reassured him.

Yogan walked towards her. 'In Veena, it's the custom to kiss a person on the cheek before they depart. Do you mind if I kiss your cheek, Lydia?' he said shyly.

'I suppose not, if it's a custom,' she smiled.

Yogan kissed Lydia's cheek and said that she could come back to Wardis House whenever she wished.

'Thank you for showing me around today,' said Lydia.

'I'll take you to Skrinkle,' he replied.

On the way back to the potion room, Lydia asked Yogan about his life.

'The Professor is our uncle, and we have lived at Wardis house since our parents were killed by the Sinaras. He's good to my brother and me, and he is teaching us to master every magic potion in the *Antikva Lektvar*, which has been a bit of a challenge,' he laughed.

'I'm sure you'll become a wonderful Spellter, Yogan,' said Lydia. 'Were there any more Spellters at Wardis?' she asked.

'Yes, Wardis House was full of apprentices and Professors,' he replied, looking pensive.

'What happened to them?' asked Lydia anxiously.

'We don't know, is the honest answer. I hope they are on the two other spheres of Veena. You see, Lydia, that fateful night, Veronians were running everywhere looking for safety; it was chaos. It was terrible,' said Yogan, looking sad.

'It must have been truly frightening, to see your world breaking apart, with so many Veronians losing their lives. And for what? Because some egotistic maniac wanted more power,' said Lydia, shaking her head in disbelief.

'My uncle the Professor ordered all Spellters of Wardis House, along with my parents, who were also Professors of magic, to head for the Lamanya Tower, for fear that Ballam and the Sinaras would destroy the sacred plinth,' Yogan explained.

'Why didn't Professor Quelldar go with them?' asked Lydia, looking confused.

'It wasn't possible. He had to stay behind at Wardis House with his servant Lutin, for fear that Ballam would destroy our home, along with the ancient book of potions,' he told her.

'The *Antikva Lektvar*,' replied Lydia.

'Ballam might have destroyed the book of potions or used it himself.' Yogan shuddered. 'Come on, let's get you back to Skrinkle.'

By the time Yogan had told Lydia about his life, they had arrived led at the potion room and saw Skrinkle and the Professor engaging in deep conversation.

'You're back, Lydia, and we must leave,' said Skrinkle, standing up from the chair.

'Before you leave, Lydia, this is for you. You will need these,' said the Professor.

He gave her a small, drawstring bag of blue velvet that contained small, round, black-coloured discs, which looked like edible rice paper.

'What's inside the bag, Professor?'' she asked.

'The Eralda Chartum. You place one of these tiny discs on your tongue and it dissolves instantly. It's quite a pleasant taste; I made the ingredients up myself,' he replied, looking quite proud of his achievements.

'But what do they do?' she asked.

'Transform you, of course, to any creature you'd like to be,' he replied.

'You mean, like a fox? No offence, Skrinkle. Even a dog or a cat?' she asked.

'Yes, Lydia, any animal or creature, but it will only work when your life is in imminent danger. You can't use them for the sake of using them, do you understand?' said the Professor.

Lydia nodded her head. 'Are they safe to take?'

'Perfectly safe! They have been used for centuries, and I have a 100 per cent success rate with my concoctions, which I'm quite proud about, even if I say so myself,' continued the Professor. 'Lady Ronan never had any problems when she took them,' he said confidently.

'When I took one of those discs I had a tail for two months,' scowled Lutin.

'Oh, I forgot about that, but Lutin, that was in the very early stages of production,' replied the Professor.

'Do you know how embarrassing it was to have a bushy tail, Professor?' said Lutin.

'*I* have a bushy tail, and it's not embarrassing at all, Lutin,' laughed Skrinkle.

'But you're a fox, Skrinkle!' Lutin gave a deep, croaky chuckle.

'I don't want to scare Lydia. They are safe, completely safe! She will need to take these if her life is in danger,' reiterated the Professor.

'Yes, I understand the importance of the Eralda Chartum discs,' said Skrinkle.

At last, having said their goodbyes to everyone at Wardis House, Lydia and Skrinkle climbed back onto their Duons, who took them to straight to the entrance of the doorway between their two worlds.

Lydia and Skrinkle took their last look at Veena, taking in its beauty, before stepping back into the dark, dank tunnel, where they waited for Veena's guardians, the Harimau tigers.

'Look, there they are!' cried Skrinkle. The tigers came bounding across the meadows before quickly jumping through the golden doorway and transforming back into black cats. Lydia and Skrinkle closed the door and locked it with the golden key.

'Never lose this key, Lydia,' said Skrinkle.

'I won't. I'll keep it safe forever,' she replied, and placed it in the zip pocket within her bag.

They made their way back through the tunnel, climbed the stone staircase, and were soon back in Lady Ronan's bedroom.

'I can't believe where I've been,' said Lydia.

'Overwhelming, I would have thought,' smiled Skrinkle.

They walked out of Lady Ronan's bedroom, closing the door behind them.

Lydia's head was all over the place. 'You know what, Skrinkle, she had a son, didn't she?' said Lydia.

' Who had a son?'

'Lady Ronan, of course!'

'Yes, she did—why are you are asking?'

'I just realised that there are no photographs of him anywhere in the castle,' she replied.

'I'm afraid that isn't quite correct. Follow me, Lydia,' said Skrinkle, as he trotted along the corridor.

'Where are we going?'

'You'll see.'

They walked to the north wing of the castle; a part that Lydia had never been to before. They arrived outside a wooden door.

'What's in there?'

Skrinkle opened the door and walked in. 'Come in, Lydia, and see for yourself. This is Edward's bedroom,' Skrinkle told her.

'There are photographs of him everywhere!' gasped Lydia.

The photographs showed Edward throughout various stages of his life, from babyhood and his teenage years into adulthood. Lydia gazed at a large portrait of a young man dressed in an army uniform sitting on a horse. With a shock she realised she had seen him before. 'Oh gosh. It's the man I saw in the woods! That's him,' Skrinkle!'

'But Edward is dead. You must be mistaken, little one. It couldn't have been *him* that you saw,' said Skrinkle.

'It was him; it was! I remember his eyes, Skrinkle! I can never tell my father that I saw his friend in the woods. He'll think I've gone mad,' she sighed.

'Come, Lydia, let's get back to your bedroom. You need to try and get some sleep. You've had an eventful time. It won't be long before you set off for Ireland,' said Skrinkle. With that, he spun around and transformed back into a fox cub.

Lydia, holding Skrinkle in her hands, crept quietly back to her bedroom and placed Skrinkle in the ottoman. Exhausted, she lay on top of her bed fully clothed, and fell asleep instantly.

Lydia finally knew Gwendonia's secrets, but never in her wildest imagination could she ever have thought that she would be taking on a quest that Lady Ronan had taken on before her.

Within a short few hours, Lydia would be leaving the castle and wouldn't be returning for several weeks. What would happen to Gwendonia while Lydia was away? Only time would tell.

Chapter 9

Strange Events In Ireland

It was time for Lydia to visit her maternal grandparents in Wexford, Ireland. She would often visit her grandparents—James and Bridget Kelly—during the holidays. However, this summer would be even more special, as Lydia would also be visiting her maternal aunt and uncle in New York City, USA. Her Aunt Evelyn and Uncle Steven Millar promised to take the family sightseeing around Manhattan during their stay. Lydia was equally excited that her cousin Grace would also be visiting New York City at the same time as the Roses. Grace lived in Middlesex, in England, and she and Lydia were very close and they would often spend the school holidays together.

'Lydia, are you all packed? We'll be leaving in the next twenty minutes,' called her mother from her bedroom a little further down the passage.

'I'm nearly finished, Mum. I just need to pack a few more items!'

'Don't take forever. We need to put your suitcase in the car. And make sure you pack appropriate clothing. Ireland can be wet, like Wales, even in the summer. You'll need your raincoat and pack plenty of T-shirts and shorts for New York too,' said her mother excitedly.

Dad came walking down the passage calling out, 'Lydia! Ellis! Do you have everything for the journey? We won't be returning for three weeks. I don't want to come back for anything.'

Ellis was in his bedroom, checking his suitcase several times to make sure he had everything. 'Dad! I'm all packed. I'll take my suitcase down to the car,' he said excitedly.

Lydia could tell that Dad and Ellis were looking forward to spending time in Ireland and visiting New York, and happy to be together as a family.

Dad popped his head round the door to check if Lydia was ready, and she saw the happiness on his face. 'Are you excited to be going on holiday?'

'I'm looking forward to seeing Ireland again, and then there's New York, New York! You know what they say,' he said excitedly, 'you've got to say it twice!'

Lydia looked at him, puzzled: she didn't have the faintest idea what he was talking about and just smiled.

'We'll have so much fun, Lydia,' he said happily.

'Yes, we will, Dad. I can't wait to see Aunt Evie and Uncle Steven. We haven't seen them in so long, it feels like forever,' said Lydia.

'We'll have two weeks with them, catching up and sightseeing. It'll be great,' said Dad, rubbing his hands. 'Shall I take your suitcase down to the car?'

'No thanks, Dad, I haven't finished packing just yet.'

'You need to get a move on, otherwise we'll miss our ferry to Rosslare.'

'I'll only be ten minutes!' She hurried to get all her packing done, feeling exhausted from the previous night's events.

Lydia's suitcase was open on top of her bed, and her clothing strewn everywhere: over her bed, on the floor, and piled up in her wardrobe. She had gone through everything, ensuring that she took enough clothing with her for three weeks. But she remembered she needed to make a little room for Skrinkle. She quickly closed her bedroom door and opened the lid of the ottoman and took out the clean white cotton bed sheets, placing them neatly in a pile on her bedroom floor.

'I've nearly got you, Skrinkle,' she whispered, as she fished around in the ottoman to where Skrinkle was sleeping.

Lydia could hear a muffled voice. 'Don't worry about me, Lydia. It's quite comfy down here, but I am not looking forward to the long journey to Ireland, stuffed away in your suitcase.'

'Ah, there you are,' cried Lydia. Skrinkle was lying at the bottom of the ottoman, on a single white bed sheet, with an enormous grin on his face.

'Come on, up you come. You'll be fine and stop moaning. I can't leave you here. I'd be scared of something happening to you while I was away. I hope you understand,' she said, gently placing him into her suitcase.

'My little one, I made a vow to Zavantos and the Veronians that I will remain by your side to guide and protect you. Everyone who lives in Veena is truly humbled that you have chosen to help us in our quest to restore our realm and fight against the sinister and the truly evil Ballam. For that, little one, I serve you until my last breath, even if it means being stuffed into a suitcase,' replied Skrinkle.

Lydia kissed the top of his head.

'Thank you, Lydia. But I hope my fur's not wet after you kissed me,' he laughed.

'Shh!' Lydia chuckled, 'they'll all hear us, especially my mother. She's only two bedrooms away' and she has ears like a bat. She can hear for miles.'

'A bat? Your mother has ears like a bat? That's very odd,' said Skrinkle. 'Let me look at you.'

'Why?'

'Hmm. Your ears look fine. Not bat-like at all. You would look rather odd with tiny ears on such a large head.'

'What are you talking about? No! She doesn't have bat ears! It's just a saying that means she's able to hear everything. So, if we are laughing, we may be caught, see? If she were to see you, I'd have to explain everything about Veena and Ballam. I'd be grounded for two years, and she'd ask about you and where you came from.'

Skrinkle's mouth was wide open, and he started to rub his head. 'If you put it like that, I won't speak. Just throw me in the suitcase, and I'll see you in Ireland.'

'I have to admit,' I did babble a bit, didn't I? Sorry,' apologised Lydia.

'Just a bit . . . actually, quite a lot! In all seriousness though, I do understand that if we are caught it puts Veena at risk,' said Skrinkle, looking sombre.

'Oh, Skrinkle, I do hope we can save Veena.'

'Yes, me too, little one. Now hurry: your father will be expecting you to be ready.'

Lydia gently closed the lid of the suitcase, locking Skrinkle inside.

Will you hurry, Lydia, please,' called Dad.

'I'm coming.' Lydia quickly grabbed her suitcase and ran down the passage to the grand staircase. As she passed the marble statues she whispered softly, 'I'll see you in a few weeks. Please look after Gran and Grandad. And the cherubs and the Woodilfs.'

Lydia walked towards the front door. The two black cats ran to her and began affectionately curling around her feet.

'Awe, Harimau! Please look after my grandparents and Gwendonia,' she whispered.

'Come on, Lydia,' called Ellis. 'Who on earth are you talking to?'

'My friends,' she replied with a smirk.

'You are odd sometimes, you really are. Come on, Mum and Dad are waiting to leave. Just think, we'll be in Ireland in a few hours,' he said excitedly. 'I can't wait to see Nanna and Granda.'

'Neither can I,' said Lydia.

Their father walked to the front door from the car. 'Thank goodness, you're finally packed! Let me put your suitcase in the car.'

Lydia's father tried grabbing the suitcase from her. 'No, it's OK Dad. I'll do it,' she responded.

'Lydia, pass me your suitcase,' said their father.

Reluctantly, she handed over the suitcase. 'Don't go throwing it, will you?' she asked.

'Whatever do you have in there?'

'Nothing special, just clothes,' she responded nervously.

'Why are you acting strange? I think you've hidden something in your case. Now tell me the truth,' he persisted. Lydia's heart was beating fast; she didn't know what to say.

'You've hidden Eggbert, haven't you?' he said, laughing.

'No, Dad, don't be silly,' she laughed with nervous relief.

The car was packed, and there was hardly any room inside the vehicle or in the boot.

This is going to be such an uncomfortable journey. We'll be squashed like sardines, Lydia told herself while getting into the back of the car.

'Move up, Lydia,' cried Ellis.

'I can't! There's nowhere to move *to!*'

The car is full of luggage, so you will have to manage,' said Mum.

As they were about to leave, Gran and Grandad came rushing to the side of the car window. 'Here you go, have these for the journey.' Gran shoved packets of boiled sweets into Lydia's and Ellis's hands.

What sweets are they Gran? I do hope they're not barley sugars, thought Lydia.

'These will help you and your brother with travel sickness. You suck on one of these and you'll both be fine all the way during the journey,' she said, smiling

'Thanks Gran,' said Lydia and Ellis, despite them both disliking the sweets immensely.

'I'm going to miss you both so much,' said Lydia, her eyes filling with tears.

'You will have a lovely time, and we'll be right here when you get back,' said Gran.

Ellis rubbed his eyes, pretending a fly had flown into it, so they he could hold back his tears.

'Have great adventures in Ireland and New York. You can both tell me all about it when you come home,' Grandad.

'We will Grandad!'

They waved enthusiastically and blew kisses to their grandparents out of the car window as car slid down to the gates of Gwendonia Castle.

'I'll see you soon, I miss you already!' Lydia shouted.

Her thoughts, however, soon returned to her time in the enchanted realm of Veena, and she wished desperately that she could tell her brother and family what had happened, but she kept everything to herself. She was afraid that something terrible would happen to them if they knew. It was a comfort, knowing that Skrinkle was packed away in her suitcase, without anyone knowing she was taking him along with her.

Lydia's maternal grandparents, James and Bridget Kelly, lived in a cottage in a small hamlet on the outskirts of Wexford Town. After several hours of travelling, the family finally arrived at Adores Cottage. Lydia smiled when she saw the cottage sign, as it was an anagram of her name and middle name, along with those of Ellis and their cousin Grace.

Their grandparents were waiting by the front door with their arms wide open, and Lydia felt overjoyed. She leapt out of the car and ran straight towards them, giving them an enormous hug.

'I've miss you so much,'' she said.

'Aye, we have miss you too,' replied Nanna and Granda. 'We are going to have the best of times over the next week. Come on in,' they smiled.

There were many tears of joy, mainly from Lydia's mother, who hadn't seen her parents for a few months. Ellis began taking the luggage from the car, throwing them by the cottage gate.

'I'll get my suitcase,' said Lydia, running towards the car.

'Suit yourself,' said Ellis.

She was fearful that Skrinkle would get hurt as the suitcase was hurled around like it was on an airport baggage carousel. Lydia took the suitcase from the boot of the car, held it up to her mouth and whispered, 'Skrinkle, it won't be long before I unpack.'

Unbeknown to Lydia, Ellis was watching her from the front door of the cottage. 'Have you gone completely mad? What have you got in there? What have you smuggled in your case? You've been acting weirder this past week or so. Let me look inside,' he chuckled.

'You dare look in my case, and I'll tell Mum and Dad about you meeting with Darcy Lugwitch in the village instead of doing your chores,' she said.

'You wouldn't dare,' he said, and feeling slightly embarrassed.

Go on, try me, I dare you.'

Lydia knew that Ellis wouldn't look in her suitcase and knowing now that she had the upper hand on her brother, she decided she would use the information to her advantage. She took her suitcase swiftly to her bedroom, locked the door, and opened her case.

'Skrinkle! Skrinkle!' she called in a soft voice.

'I'm OK. I've slept most of the way.' He began pushing clothing aside with his paws until Lydia could finally see his face.

'Please can you get me something to eat,' he said, 'and a little water would be heavenly.'

126

'Yes, of course,' she replied, and off she went to the kitchen. She returned with a small plate of food and a bowl of water.

Skrinkle was still sitting in the suitcase, waiting patiently. He devoured every single crumb of food and climbed on the bed to where Lydia was seated. He noticed the worry on Lydia's face and knew what was troubling her. 'What you are doing is extremely brave, little one. I am also afraid of what lies ahead for us both. But, you know, you were chosen for a reason. I believe that all of Veena, including Ezra, Seraphina, and Celeste, will be looking over us to protect us and keep us safe.'

Lydia nodded her head while looking blankly at the wall. 'I know. I am quite frightened of what might be coming. We can talk about this later, but now I must go downstairs, otherwise; they'll be wondering where I am.'

'You go. I'll be fine. I'll hide until you return,' said Skrinkle.

'Thank you, I'll be as quick as I can. And don't go transforming—stay as a fox cub. It makes a noise when you transform into an adult fox,' she laughed.

'I won't. Now go and see your family.'

Lydia went into the kitchen. All the family had congregated there, and were telling stories and discussing the recent events regarding the late Lady Ronan and inheriting Gwendonia castle.

'Isn't that grand? You have an impressive castle all to yourself,' said Granda. 'Us two will need to come and pay ya a visit.'

'Please come, that would be brilliant. You can stay with us forever, or for as long as you like,' said Lydia, who was worried about the Sinaras potentially harming her grandparents. She wanted all the family to be protected somehow.

'I'll tell ya what—when you come back from New York, we'll come and visit. OK?' said Nanna.

Lydia and Ellis nodded their heads and began beaming at the thought of their grandparents coming to stay with them at the castle. Lydia sat by the kitchen table, thinking about the realm and the quest ahead of her. Her was interrupted by the sound of the family making their way to the living room.

'What's wrong, Lydia? You've looked a little worried since you've arrived. Tell me all ya troubles, and I'll see if I can fix them,' said Nanna, as she put her arms around Lydia.

'I'm fine, Nanna, really I am. I'm just happy to see you and Granda, that's all,' said Lydia.

'Well, I don't believe ya. I know when something is troubling ya,' Nanna persisted.

'I'm tired, that's all, Nanna.'

'You need to have a good night's sleep, and then you and your brother can take yourselves off down to the beach tomorrow. I know how much you love being close to the sea, and I'll make you Irish rarebit when you come back,' she said, smiling. 'You do know I am well known in these parts as the best cook. I guess it's the secret ingredients that I throw in,' said Nanna, looking rather proud of herself.

Lydia looked up at Nanna and gave her a slight smile.

'Now, drink up your hot chocolate and off to bed with ya! It's been a long day for you.'

Lydia walked upstairs, with Ellis following soon after. 'Goodnight!' they shouted to each other before going into their bedrooms.

'Goodnight!' the rest of the family yelled from the living room.

Lydia saw Skrinkle lying at the bottom of the bed, curled up and fast asleep again. Lydia wanted to talk to him about their quest to restore Veena, but she couldn't wake him up, and he looked so peaceful, she let him be. She made sure she locked her bedroom door from the inside so that no one could suddenly come in and see him lying there.

Morning came. Lydia woke slowly and though her eyes were closed, knew that someone was watching her. As she slowly opened her eyes, she saw that it was Skrinkle, sitting with his head tilted to the side, looking at her.

'Morning, Skrinkle! Did you sleep well?' she asked.

'Yes, I did. It must be the Irish air,' he chuckled.

Lydia told Skrinkle her plans for the day ahead. Following breakfast, the family would be going into town for several hours, while Lydia and Ellis would be going to the beach. 'You'll have the place to yourself. You can roam around, go out in the garden, and get yourself something to eat. But don't make a mess, as Nanna will know. She has everything in order and doesn't like anything out of place,' said Lydia. 'Ellis and I are going to wander down to the beach. We shouldn't be too long. I'd rather go to the beach than go shopping for hours,' she smiled.

'Keep safe, Lydia. You know that evil is all around, and remember what Zavantos told you about Ballam's servants, the Sinaras. They could be anywhere. Keep your wits about you, and always remain vigilant,' he told her.

'Do you think the Sinaras would be in Ireland?' she asked.

'Maybe, I don't know, Lydia. All I know is that Ballam's been wandering around this earth plane for centuries. The Sinaras could be anywhere, looking to stop anyone trying to defeat them and their master,' he said with a sullen look.

'I'll see you later. You keep safe too, and hide if anyone knocks the door,' she told him. Lydia walked out of the bedroom and made her way downstairs. All the family were in the kitchen, sitting by the breakfast table.

'Are you both looking forward to going down to the beach?' asked Nanna.

'I am, Nanna,' said Lydia excitedly.

'Beach? What's this about going to the beach? I'm not going; I don't fancy it at all. I'll stay here, if that's OK,' said Ellis.

'No, it's not OK Ellis,' said Grandad. 'You'll go with your sister to the beach, or you will come into town with us shopping. It's your choice.'

'Not much of a choice really. I'll go with Lydia then,' he said, frowning.

Ellis's parents and grandparents laughed. 'Oh come on, Ellis. You're on holiday! Go and explore with your sister,' said Dad.

Mum rummaged through her leather purse and handed money to Ellis. 'Here we go. There's some money for you both to get ice cream and a drink. It'll be around 12:30pm, so make sure you're back by then for lunch.'

'We'll be back on time, we promise. Thanks for the money,' said Ellis. The children got up from their chairs, put on their shoes, and ran out of the cottage towards the beach.

Lydia always loved visiting Wexford beach. 'Hurry Ellis, faster, come on!' she yelled. Soon they found themselves standing in the tall grass, among the rocks that hugged the craggy coastline. It was a warm morning and a gentle summer breeze was blowing the grass against their bare legs.

'It's a lot like Wales, don't you think,' Ellis?' she asked.

'What is?'

'Ireland. It's very similar.'

'If you say it is,' he said, not in the slightest bit interested

'What's the point in talking to you? Look, Ellis. Look! There's Darcy,'' she cried, pointing straight ahead.

'Where is she? I can't see her,' Ellis replied excitedly.

'I don't know, Wales probably,' she laughed.

'Will you stop messing around!'

'What would Darcy be doing in Ireland?' She wouldn't be following you, would she?'

'Shut up, Lydia. It's only 10am and already you're getting on my nerves.'

'I hope you're not going to be a complete bore during the holidays. You used to have a laugh, but lately you've become all serious, Ellis.'

'Come on, we'll climb down the rocks instead of taking the steps down to the beach,' said Ellis smiling, trying to cheer her up.

'It looks really steep,' she said. They gazed down from the top of the cliff to where the huge rock sank deep into the sand below.

'I don't want to fall and break my neck just because you think it's quicker to climb down the rocks,' she moaned.

'I'll help you. You're not going to fall. Just hold my hand, OK?''

Ellis grabbed Lydia's hand and began treading on the rocks carefully, stopping to check their balance every few seconds. Finally, with a little jump onto the soft sand, they were at the bottom. 'See, I told you it was safe. It isn't dangerous at all; It's just quicker,' said Ellis.

He began peering inside the crevice of the large the rock. 'Gross, just gross! Don't look inside Lydia, it's too gruesome,' he shuddered. Lydia thought that Ellis was trying to frighten her and dismissed his warning. She looked inside the crevice and couldn't believe what she was seeing.

'Oh no, what have they done to it, Ellis?' she cried.

'I told you not to look didn't I?' said Ellis, as he tried to console his sister. Hidden within the crevice was a mutilated fox.

There were clumps of fur clinging to the sharp edges of the rock. It was horrifying. Lydia immediately thought of Skrinkle and knew that she had to protect him, even though he was sent to protect her.

Ellis tried to cheer up his sister. 'Let's walk up the beach. It goes on for miles, but we'd better keep an eye on the time, otherwise we'll miss lunch and Nanna won't be happy. Come on, I'll race you.'

Before Lydia had the chance to answer, Ellis was sprinting up the beach. Lydia tried doing her very best to catch up with him, and while she was running, she thought of every possible thing that could stop her brother from winning the race.

'Ellis! Look, it's a jellyfish!' she shouted.

Ellis stopped running and looked back, confused. He jogged to Lydia to see what had caught her attention. 'It looks dead. I don't want—' Before Ellis could finish the sentence' Lydia had picked up a handful of seaweed and threw it at his head.

'Lydia! No, no! That's not funny at all!' he shouted.

'Oh, but it is, Ellis. You look like a sea creature,' she laughed, holding her hands on her stomach.

'You think it's funny, do you?' he said, and began picking the seaweed from his head and throwing it hard onto the sand before walking off, Lydia trailing behind and giggling to herself.

'Look, Lydia—here's are some shells for your art,' he said, and began picking up something in his hand.

Before Lydia could see what it was that he had picked up, he threw a crab's skeleton at her. 'Lovely shell, isn't it?' he laughed.

Lydia was frantic, trying to get the crab skeleton off her without touching it. 'Get it off! Get it off!' In all the commotion, with Lydia screaming and Ellis laughing, they hadn't noticed three children on top of the rocks and glaring at them. The children turned away and walked off when Lydia and Ellis finally saw them.

'That's a bit odd. Oh well, come on, let's go back,' said Ellis. 'Don't go throwing any more seaweed at me, Lyd. I smell like a tin of tuna as it is,' he laughed.

'I won't, I promise,' she giggled.

Lydia and Ellis started making their way home, chatting as they went. At that moment, Lydia spotted four adults standing by the rocks, looking directly at them, their faces emotionless. It made Lydia feel uneasy, but Ellis was oblivious. 'Lyd, let's climb those rocks again. It'll be quicker to go home that way,' he suggested.

'No, can we go the long way around instead?' she asked, trying to avoid passing the four adults.

Ellis could not understand why Lydia would want to take the longer route. However, he went along with Lydia's suggestion. She felt relieved that Ellis had agreed, and they finally found themselves back on the path by the craggy rocks.

They stopped at the ice cream kiosk. Lydia walked to the edge of the rocks and looked down to see if the four adults were still there, but they had vanished. Her eyes wandered over the pristine sandy beach, but no, they were gone. *Where could they have gone?* she thought.

Lydia had become paranoid ever since Zavantos had spoken about the evilness of the Sinaras and their ability to transform into normal-looking human beings. She became overwhelmed with fear and thought of explaining the situation to Ellis, who was walking towards her holding two ice cream cones.

Lydia was bursting to tell her brother about Skrinkle and the enchanted world beneath Gwendonia. 'Ellis, I want to tell you something.'

'What is it?' he asked, while passing Lydia an ice cream cone.

At the last moment she changed her mind. 'Who do you think those children were? They looked at us oddly, didn't they?'

'Who cares! Don't worry about it. We were having a laugh, that's all. They looked miserable anyway,' he said. 'Come on, lunch will be ready and we're on time, for once.'

They walked through the cottage gate and were greeted by Nanna. 'There you are! You're just in time. Please go and wash your hands.'

Lydia and Ellis rushed to the bathroom and quickly washed their hands before returning to the kitchen table.

'Come on, I've made plenty for you all, so tuck in,' said Nanna, as she dished out the food. The family began talking about their day, and especially about Ellis's and Lydia's morning at the beach.

'Yeah, it wasn't too bad. I enjoyed it,' said Ellis.

'It was good. I'd probably go there again soon. But we did see something gruesome in the rock crevice. It was a dead fox. It was so upsetting. Ellis was nice to me, and told me not to look,' said Lydia.

'I'm glad that you pair had a good morning, apart from the fox, and that you're not bickering at each other for once. Thank you, Ellis, for taking care of your sister,' said Dad.

Nanna got up from the table and started looking around the kitchen. 'Does anyone know where all the fruit has gone? I'm sure there was plenty in the fruit bowl this morning,' she said, looking puzzled. The glass fruit bowl, in the centre of the kitchen table, was completely empty. Lydia was certain that it must have been Skrinkle who had eaten all the fruit and quickly told Nanna, 'I took some with me today, for the beach, so did Ellis, didn't you?' she said, staring pleadingly at her brother.

'What?'

'Fruit, Ellis. You had some this morning,' she said, her eyes widening.

'Did I?'

'Yes, you did.'

Ellis looked at Lydia with a confused expression, knowing that neither of them had taken fruit from the bowl.

'I can fill it up for you later, if you'd like, Nanna,' said Lydia. Ellis looked at her, knowing that she was lying,'but he didn't say anything. She didn't dare tell her family that it was Skrinkle, the enchanted fox, who had devoured the entire contents of the fruit bowl; how could she?

Once everyone had finished their lunch, they went out into the garden, apart from Lydia and Nanna, who continued chatting by the kitchen table.

'What was the beach like today?' Nanna asked.

'It was lovely. It was only Ellis and me, apart from a woman walking a little boy, oh and four adults, who looked a bit odd,' she continued.

'What do ya mean by odd?' Nanna chuckled.

'They weren't talking and looked scary,' replied Lydia.

'Perhaps they were enjoying the scenery at that beautiful beach,' said Nanna. 'You've been going to that beach since you were born. Granda and I would take you for long walks in your pram. What lovely times there were too.'

'I wish you lived closer, Nanna,' said Lydia.

'We're only a little way across the water, and we are connected by an invisible thread that's sewn into our hearts. It connects us to one another, wherever we are in the world. The thread can never break; it's powerful and remains attached to our hearts for all eternity. What it means, Lydia, is that you are very much loved. All you need to do is think of us, and we will always be with you,' said Nanna, holding Lydia's hand.

'I love you so much, I just miss not being able to see you and Granda every day,' said Lydia. 'We love you and we'll be coming to stay with you for a while when you return from New York,' she smiled. 'I can't wait, Nanna,' said Lydia, smiling.

Then Lydia remembered the three children they had seen while they were at the beach, and told Nanna. 'They were on top of the rocks, looking down at Ellis and me.'

'Why they're Lord and Lady Kavanagh's children: Phineas, Verity, and Ophelia. They spend a lot of time in New York and Switzerland, as they have relatives in both countries. They must be spending time at home, as it's the school holidays. They are lovely children,' said Nanna.

'Lovely? They looked miserable, not a smile on their faces,' replied Lydia, rolling her eyes.

'Oh, give them a chance! You'll like them once you get to know them,' said Nanna.

'I don't want to get to know them Nanna, thank you.'

'Oh, don't say that Lydia. They are nice children. I'll tell you what, I'll contact Mrs Tolsdale, the housekeeper, to arrange for you and Ellis to visit Abban Manor and introduce yourselves to the Kavanagh children,' said Nanna.

'It's OK, you don't have to do that,' replied Lydia.

Lydia's grandmother wasn't having any of it: she was going to ensure that Lydia and Ellis met the children at Abban Manor, despite Lydia's reluctance. There was no use in Lydia trying to negotiate with her grandmother—once she had made up her mind it was set in stone.

'How do you know the family, Nanna?' asked Lydia.

'Long before you and your brother were born, I was the head housekeeper at Abban Manor for the late Lord Kavanagh. I was 16 years old when I began working at the manor,' she explained.

'What was it like working there?'

'I worked there for over forty years, until I retired. It was just before your brother was born. Therefore, I can safely say that you'll like the Kavanagh children because, occasionally, I still visit the manor, and I know the children personally,' she continued. 'Abban Manor is a grand old building, but only if the walls could talk. They'd tell you many secrets, no doubt.' she smirked.

Lydia was intrigued by what Nanna told her: what did she mean about the manor having secrets, she asked?

'I worked there for many years and saw strange things happening that no one could explain,' said Nanna, looking a little afraid.

'Strange things? Like what?' said Lydia, thinking that nothing could be as strange as what she had encountered at Gwendonia castle.

'There would be lots of banging, but nobody knew where it was coming from. And there was an occasion when I was—'

Before Nanna could explain any further, there was a knock on the front door. Nanna stood up from the chair and went to answer it; it was her neighbour, Mrs Roberts. Lydia sat at the kitchen table giggling, as she could see and hear Nanna and Mrs Roberts gossiping by the front door.

Suddenly, Lydia's face turned white. She couldn't move. Slowly walking past Adores cottage were the four adults from the beach. Lydia could see them gazing at Nanna and Mrs Roberts. Their faces were expressionless and they didn't speak a word. Lydia ran upstairs and closed her bedroom door behind her. Quickly, she picked up the Lamanya Stone. 'It's moving Skrinkle, look, it's warning us,' said Lydia, breathing heavily.

Skrinkle jumped up onto the windowsill and began peering outside. 'I can't see anyone.'

Lydia told him about the four adults from the beach, who had just passed the cottage only moments ago. She looked again at the Lamanya Stone. 'It's not moving now, its peaceful. For now, we're out of danger. They're in Ireland, Skrinkle, I know it,' said Lydia, looking stony-faced.

'I fear you may be right,' said Skrinkle, shaking his head.

Now Lydia would have to be on her guard against the evil Sinaras lurking in Ireland, as well as being made to visit Abban Manor, as arranged by her grandmother, knowing the sole purpose of the visit was to meet the loathsome Kavanagh children. However, she had an overwhelming urge to explore this grand old building that, she now knew, held many secrets. But most of all, she was eager to have the visit over and done with: she had more disturbing issues on her mind and wasn't looking to make new friends, especially after having observed the Kavannaghs' unfriendly demeanour at the beach earlier that morning.

Chapter 10

The Enchanted Lauma

Lydia thought about nothing else except the four strangers she had seen at the beach and outside Adores cottage the day before. She was afraid that they were Ballam's servants, the Sinaras. When no one was looking, she would take the Lamanya Stone from her pocket and check it to see if there was any movement within the stone.

She thought also about Abban Manor and what Nanna had told her about the strange events that had happened there when she was housekeeper. She desperately wanted to visit the manor before leaving Ireland for New York.

'Lydia! Ellis! Would you come in here, please!' Nanna called. When they were in the living room she told them that she had arranged with Mrs Tolsdale, Abban Manor's housekeeper, for them to visit there the following day.

'Do we have to go, Nanna?' asked Ellis.

'Yes, you do! It won't hurt you to go and meet the children, Ellis. You won't be there long.'

Ellis looked miserable: he didn't want to visit Abban Manor and preferred spending time with his grandparents.

'I told Mrs Tolsdale that you'll be there by 1.30,' said Nanna, making her way into the kitchen.

'I don't want to go, Lyd, do you?' moaned Ellis.

'Not really, but Nanna told me that when she worked at the manor, strange things happened, so I just want to visit the building. I'm not bothered about making friends. We'll have to visit Ellis, even if it's only for ten minutes.'

'I know we do, but doesn't it seem pointless?'

'I suppose so. We'll just get it over and done with tomorrow.'

At that moment, Nanna called Lydia into the kitchen and asked her if she would pop into town on an errand.

'Yes, I'll go, Nanna!'

'You're a good girl! Here's the money for the groceries, and get yourself some sweets.'

'Thank you, Nanna! I won't be too long. Ellis, do you want to come into town?' shouted Lydia.

'No thanks, I'll stay here, but you can bring me back some sweets if you like,' he replied.

'Suit yourself—stay here and be boring. And no, I won't be bringing you back any sweets,'' she yelled.

She ran upstairs to her bedroom and grabbed her bag. 'Skrinkle, Skrinkle, where are you?' she whispered.

'I'm here, on the windowsill,' a little voice called out.

'What are you doing there? What if someone saw you?

'It's lovely and warm here in the sunlight. It's quite snuggly,' he yawned.

'You'll get caught if you don't move. Come on, you're coming into town with me.'

Lydia picked up Skrinkle from the windowsill and placed him into her bag. Before they left the house, Skrinkle asked, 'Do you have the Lamanya Stone? And the transformation discs?'

'Yes, yes, they're in my bag'.

'Good girl! But what about the Golden Key, and the Diamond Angel?'

'In my bag too, Skrinkle; in a zipped pocket, so they can't fall out. Will you stop worrying? They're perfectly safe.'

'I do panic, because I need to make sure that you have everything to keep yourself safe. They could be anywhere, those evil Sinaras.'

'I know you worry, but I don't believe they'll be in Wexford Town.'

'Then who were the four adults you saw yesterday: the ones at the beach and outside the cottage? You need to remember to never become complacent—never. Do you understand?'

'I do, I do. Now, we need to go, so stop talking until we leave the cottage,' begged Lydia.

'What are we waiting for? I'm excited to see the town and all those lovely Irish people you've told me all about,' he smiled.

Lydia hurried down the stairs with Skrinkle tucked safely inside the bag slung over her shoulder. Lydia's mother heard her running down the stairs. 'Be careful! No talking to strangers—straight there and back. No dawdling.'

'OK, Mum, I'll be as quick as I can,' she replied.

Lydia and Skrinkle made their way into town. Skrinkle poked his head out of the top of her bag and they began to chat. Lydia told him that she and Ellis would be visiting Abban Manor the following day.

'My nanna wants us to introduce ourselves to the Kavanagh children,' she sighed.

'What's wrong with that? It might be fun! You might make new friends, and that's always a good thing, Lydia. You can meet up with them every time you visit Ireland,' said Skrinkle.

'They didn't look friendly at all when Ellis and I saw them at the beach. They just stared at us and walked off,' she replied.

'Give them a chance; they might turn out to be nice, once you get to know them.'

'If they're prickly when we meet them tomorrow, I certainly won't be going back to Abban Manor, no matter what my nanna may say,' said Lydia firmly.

'You'll be fine. I'm sure they are lovely children.'

'We'll soon see.' Lydia still wasn't convinced.

When they arrived in Wexford Town, Skrinkle peered out of the bag and gazed around.

'It's lovely,' isn't it?' said Lydia. 'But be very careful that you are not seen, as I know a lot of the shop owners, who know my nanna and granda, and they'll tell them I had a fox cub in my bag.'

'Lovely! It's simply a lovely town. I'll be careful, don't worry about me,' replied Skrinkle smiling.

Firstly, Lydia went to the bakery shop and told Skrinkle to hide. 'Afternoon,' Mr O'Connor, please may I have a large, uncut tin loaf?'

'Hello Lydia, how lovely to see you! On holidays at your nanna and granda's, are you?' he asked, smiling.

Lydia had known Mr O'Connor since she was a small child as he was a friend of Lydia's grandparents. He was a good-natured gentleman, tall and imposing, with wavy ginger hair and a long ginger beard, a strong Irish accent and a deep voice. You could always hear him either whistling or singing traditional Irish tunes in his shop.

'Yes, it's lovely to be back. I'm here for the week, then off to New York for two weeks to visit Auntie Evelyn and Uncle Steven,' she told him excitedly. Lydia's aunt and uncle had owned a cake shop in Wexford Town before they'd emigrated to New York.

'Sounds fantastic! Give my love to them. We do miss them in the town. How long have they been living in New York? Time has gone so quickly, Lydia!'

'Five years now. I can't wait to see them,' she said excitedly.

'I bet they'll be just as excited to see you too, Lydia. Here we go, one tin loaf. It's a bit warm— it's not long out of the oven.'

'Thank you very much, Mr O'Connor,' she replied.

Lydia paused to inhale the delicious smell of baked bread then eased the warm loaf carefully into her bag so as not to squash Skrinkle.

'This is for you, Lydia!' shouted out Mr O'Connor.

'What is it?' she asked.

'A fresh jam doughnut, as I haven't seen you in ages. Give my regards to your parents and grandparents.'

'I will! Thank you again. See you soon!'

Once outside the bakery shop, Lydia looked in her bag and saw Skrinkle sitting at the bottom, looking up at her.

'He was a lovely man, wasn't he?' said Skrinkle.

'I told you the people in Ireland were lovely, didn't I?' she smiled. 'Now I need to buy butter, and then some sweets, and then we can make our way home.'

The dairy shop was just around the corner from Mr O'Connor's bakery. As she headed for the dairy, Lydia was very conscious of anyone that might be looking at her and kept a close watch out for anyone suspicious. Once at the shop, she quickly opened the door and stepped in. 'Hello Mrs Hall,' she called out.

'Hello, hello Lydia, what can I get you?' she asked.

'A tub of butter, please,' she replied. Mrs Hall placed the butter on the counter while Lydia got out her purse to pay. She handed the money to Mrs Hall quickly, as other customers were waiting to be served, and they exchanged goodbyes before leaving the shop.

Next stop was the sweet shop, which was jam-packed with glass jars full to the brim of every sweet you could imagine. 'I don't know what to buy! I was certain I was going to get lemon sherbet drops,' she whispered to Skrinkle, while continuing to ponder.

As Lydia looked in the shop window, Skrinkle appeared from her bag. He became anxious and started to look around, studying the townspeople.

'What are you doing? Put your head back in the bag; you'll be seen,' Lydia hissed.

Skrinkle didn't listen, but continued looking around anxiously. He'd noticed that two women were standing on the opposite side of the road, their eyes fixed on Lydia, neither moving nor talking to one another. Lydia, still salivating over the sweets in the sweet shop, was oblivious.

'I don't want you to panic, but the angels inside the Lamanya Stone appear to be warning us. I don't want you to turn around—do you understand?

'What are you talking about?

'Do you see them? The two women—look in the reflection in the window,' he told her. Lydia saw the two women looking directly at her. They were wearing summer dresses and had long, straight, black hair. Their faces were expressionless. Lydia instantly knew it was the Sinaras. 'It's them, isn't it, Skrinkle?' she said, terrified. 'They know who I am; they know my family is in Ireland, don't they?'

'You need to trust me, little one, and do as I tell you.'

'But I can't move. I'm too afraid of what they'll do to me,' she replied.

'When I say run, you will need to run and follow my instructions, understand? You can't stand here looking in the shop window. You'll need to run and run as fast as you can.

'I understand,' she replied.

'Boo!' It was Ellis, jumping up on her back. Lydia leapt away in fright before she realised it was her brother. 'What's wrong with you? she cried, her heart racing.

'What's wrong with *you*? You look as though you've seen a ghost. Sorry if I scared you,' he giggled.

'What are you doing here?'

Ellis took a deep breath. 'Mum told me to come and make sure that you were OK that's all. You still look quite scared. You OK?'

'No, not really,' she answered, looking around nervously.

'What's wrong with you?'

'Don't turn around Ellis, please. Please look in the shop window. Do you notice two women on the opposite side of the road looking directly at me? They might want to harm me or even kill me. I'm sure of it.'

'Do you know how mad you sound? They look completely normal to me. Why on earth would they want to kill you?' he said, his eyebrows raised.

'You'd never believe me if I told you what has happened. No one would.'

'Try me.'

'I'm sorry to interrupt you both, but we need to get out of here as quickly as we can,' said Skrinkle.

'What's that? Who's that talking in your bag?' he stammered.

'It's Skrinkle'

'Skrinkle? What's that?' he said, taking a step back in shock.

'Trust me, Ellis, please,' she pleaded.

'Ready? One, two, three: Run! Run!' yelled Skrinkle.

Lydia grabbed Ellis's arm and dragged him with her. 'Run, Ellis, run! Please listen to me!' she begged. 'Where are we going, Skrinkle?' shouted Lydia, as they continued to run as fast as they could.

'To the woods! Head for the woods,' Skrinkle shouted, as they ran out of the town.

Ellis looked over his shoulder and noticed that the two women were chasing them. 'You're right—they're running behind us! Don't stop running. They're coming after us,' he cried.

Skrinkle yelled at Lydia and Ellis. 'Head for the oak tree; it's in the centre of the woods. You can't miss it.'

'A tree! Head for a tree!' screamed Lydia,

'What's a tree going to do? There are trees everywhere— we're in the woods.'

'Just trust me,' Skrinkle yelled. Lydia and Ellis zig-zagged through the woods, trying to lose the two women chasing them, turning back only to see how close the women were behind them.

They were no longer being chased by the women they had seen earlier; they were different creatures now, their faces morphing into the most grotesque facial features they had ever seen. The creatures looked like something out of the most terrible of nightmares. They were skeleton-like, with straight, jet-black hair; black, sunken eyes; and protruding cheekbones. Long, spidery fingers reached out from bony arms, desperately trying to grab at them. Lydia and Ellis had never in their lives been so frightened.

'They're getting closer!' screamed Lydia. She was exhausted and had begun to slow down.

'Don't stop running, Lydia!' Ellis grabbed her arm and started pulling her along with him.

'I'm so tired,' Ellis,' she moaned, trying to keep pace with her brother.

'You can do this, little one. We're nearly there!' cried Skrinkle.

Behind them, amid the trees, they heard screams and the sound of chanting. It was the Sinaras. *We'll kill all who stand in Ballam's way, we walk amongst you every day, be it night or day we never sleep, Taros our realm is where we'll reap.*

I'm freaking out! What are those things? Who is Ballam? We don't know a Ballam!' Ellis shouted at them.

The Sinaras appeared to be floating in the air, cackling and screaming in the most menacing of voices. 'We are going to kill you! Stop running! You can't get away.'

'We haven't done anything wrong. We don't know who you are!' Ellis yelled while running faster and dragging Lydia along with Skrinkle, who was still in Lydia's bag.

'The Mudum Lupus are with the Sinaras,' shouted Skrinkle.

'What are the Mudum Lupus?' said Lydia.

'Don't look behind you, Lydia; just run as fast as you can,' Ellis demanded.

Lydia, as curious as ever, didn't listen to her brother and looked over her shoulder. What she saw was a pack of snarling, vicious, black creatures frothing from their mouths as they raced towards her.

'They're wolves!' she screamed.

'Lydia! Ellis! Keep running! Run straight in front of you. Head for that glowing oak tree—it's the Lauma!' yelled Skrinkle.

In front of them lay an enormous oak tree with a massive trunk that sat above tall, thick, and twisted roots, illuminated by many tiny specks of light that winked and glittered amid the dense greenery.

'Run up the roots and look for a face in the tree trunk!' Skrinkle yelled.

'A face on a tree? This is getting worse every second!' shouted out Ellis.

Lydia and Ellis hurled themselves at the tree with the Sinaras and their wolves just feet away from them. At that moment, a beautiful female face appeared on the tree trunk. The face fixed its gaze on the Sinaras and the Mudum Lupus.

'Goddess Lauma, open for us!' shouted out Skrinkle.

Terrified, Lydia and Ellis saw the mouth of the goddess open wide.

'Jump inside!' Skrinkle ordered.

Ellis jumped first, holding on to Lydia. He landed inside the hollow trunk but his sister did not follow: her head and torso were inside the goddess's mouth but her legs were being pulled by the Sinaras, and she screamed in agony as they clawed at her. Ellis quickly stood up from the trunk floor and began pulling his sister with all his might.

The Sinaras howled horribly from outside. 'Let go! Stop trying to save your sister. She'll soon perish and then it'll be your turn.'

'You'll never have my sister!' screamed Ellis, holding onto Lydia. He could hear the wolves outside, snarling and snapping at poor Lydia. Suddenly, a wolfish snout dripping with drool appeared through the entrance and snapped at Ellis's arm as he clung to Lydia. It took a chunk out of him. Ellis screamed in pain and blood ran down his arm and onto the floor of the tree trunk hollow.

'Don't let go Ellis, please!' Lydia screamed. Ellis gritted his teeth and despite the pain and exhaustion he clung on, though he knew he wouldn't be able to do so for long, and that the hideous creatures outside would claim him and his sister. Skrinkle's voice was bellowing from inside Lydia's bag, 'Hold on! More help is coming!'

Outside, the Sinaras mocked. 'Skrinkle! Skrinkle! That interfering fox won't be able to help you, you foolish girl. He couldn't even save his own people!'

Suddenly, Ellis heard a piercing, screeching sound coming from outside the tree. He couldn't see what was making such a deafening sound.

'What's happening Lydia!' he cried out.

Lydia, writhing in the Sinaras' clutches, twisted her head and saw a look of terror in the awful faces of her attackers. A thunderous noise was approaching them.

'There's something coming and the Sinaras look scared. It's flying towards us!' Lydia screamed.

Ellis summoned every ounce of energy that he had left and pulled hard on Lydia's arms. Distracted, the Sinaras had loosened their grip, and Lydia flew from their grasp and fell into the tree on top of her brother. The mouth of the goddess closed immediately above them. 'You're safe now, Lydia,' said Ellis, cuddling his sister as she sobbed in his arms.

He looked down at his arm and sister's legs: they were both covered in blood. Ellis took off his T-shirt and tore off the bottom part to make bandages, which he wrapped around Lydia's legs.

'What the hell is going on?' he said, shaking with fright. He looked around. The inside of the tree had wooden seats carved into it, and it was lit up by glass jars full of fireflies.

'We just jumped through a woman's face and now we're inside a tree!' Ellis stammered.

'It was her mouth we jumped into,' replied Lydia quietly as she sat on the wooden seat, her face stained with tears.

'Face, mouth, whatever: does it matter? This is not real. It can't be real.'

'It is real, Ellis. We're safe in here though,' she told him.

'Safe? Are you kidding me? We've been chased through the woods by ugly Halloween creatures chanting some crazy rhyme, and a pack of dogs, and then you have some talking thing in your bag that's been giving us directions!' ranted Ellis. 'You'd better tell me what's going on, Lydia. Otherwise, I'll be telling Mum and Dad. That's if we ever make it out of here alive.'

'They weren't dogs; they were wolves,' Lydia replied.

'Does it matter? Dogs or wolves—they have huge teeth and lots of them. I know because they bit me. They would have killed and eaten us!'

Lydia and Ellis could still hear the haunting screams and yelps from outside the tree. Ellis and Lydia were still petrified: even though they were safe in the tree, they didn't know what was going on outside.

'Who's in your bag, Lydia?' demanded Ellis.

'Just shut up for a minute Ellis, will you, please.'

Suddenly, the tree started shaking violently. Ellis and Lydia tried to hold on to the wooden seats but fell onto the tree trunk floor, where they were tossed around. Piercing screams and screeches could still be heard coming from outside. The screams and yells were so loud that Lydia and Ellis tried to cover their ears with their hands; it was so frightening. After several minutes, the screams began to fade until finally there was silence. It was eerily quiet. Lydia and Ellis got up off the floor and sat back onto the seats.

'Are you all right?' called out Skrinkle from inside the bag.

'I think it's time I met whoever you have in your bag, Lydia,' said Ellis.

'Yes, I think you're right.' Lydia put her two hands inside her bag and pulled out Skrinkle.

'It's a fox cub! But it was talking and telling us where to go,' said Ellis, bewildered. 'Foxes can't talk, so why is this one talking?'

Lydia placed Skrinkle on the floor and asked him to transform. 'Let's really freak him out, Skrinkle.'

Skrinkle span around quickly, just as he had done in the tunnel. After several seconds, he was transformed. '*Voila*! Hello Ellis, I'm Skrinkle and I come from the realm of Veena. I am guarding your sister on her quest to restore our world and destroy Ballam and his servants, the Sinaras, whom you've just had the unfortunate opportunity to meet.'

Ellis listened, still as a statue, as Skrinkle told them that the screams they had heard had come from the Sinaras and Mudum

Lupus, and that the enchanted Lauma and the winged Esmaga had destroyed them.

'I saw the winged Esmaga. Its wings were gigantic and black in colour, and its body like that of a panther, with a human like face peering from behind black feathers. It looked terrifying', said Lydia.

'I'm glad they're on our side Lydia', Skrinkle replied.

'Yes, me too. No wonder the Sinaras looked terrified'.

'How did those people turn into such horrible creatures?' asked Ellis.

'They are odium morphs and can change into humans, and that is why it is so difficult to know their whereabouts, Ellis. They walk among us like ordinary people.'

'They want to kill Skrinkle and anyone who helps him or the Veronians,' said Lydia.

'You see, Ellis, your sister, is the one chosen to help us,' Skrinkle proudly explained.

'My sister? Are you sure you have the right person? No offence, Lydia.'

'Yes, really. Your sister is braver and stronger than you realise, my friend. We will face many perilous dangers on our quest.'

'What, like this one? With those creatures trying to kill you, my sister, and now me?'

'Ballam has an army of Sinaras. They are his servants, who will die in their quest to ensure that he lives and returns to his realm, Taros. Should this happen, he will enslave us or destroy Veena,' said Skrinkle.

Lydia and Skrinkle told Ellis everything about Lady Ronan, her ancestors, the enchanted realm of Veena, and the magical secrets of Gwendonia.

Ellis sat there in amazement. 'I'm sorry, Lydia, for thinking that you had gone mad, but you were acting so differently since Lady Ronan died. I understand now. You kept a lot to yourself, and that must have been really hard.'

'I wanted to tell you so many times, Ellis, I really did, but I was afraid. I didn't want to put you or the family in danger,' she told him.

'I'm sorry, but I'm going to have to help you now, if that's OK,' he smiled.

Lydia got up from the bench and hugged her brother. 'Thank you, thank you.'

'A difficult and dangerous journey lies ahead for us: it's only a matter of time before Ballam knows that two of his servants have been destroyed in Ireland. There may be many more on their way, I fear,' said Skrinkle.

'The adults we saw at the beach maybe they were Sinaras too,' said Lydia.

'What's the plan?' asked Ellis.

'We need to fix your sister's legs before we leave the safety of the goddess Lauma,' said Skrinkle. He reached into his coat pocket and took out the smallest, teeniest glass jar full of what looked like tiny pearls.

'What is it, Skrinkle?' asked Lydia.

'These, little one, are called Ora pearls, and they will heal you,' he explained, as he sprinkled them all over the cuts and scratches on her legs.

'Ora pearls?' asked Ellis inquisitively.

'Yes, they are healing pearls; they can heal most things,' smiled Skrinkle.

Lydia and Ellis watched in amazement as the blood, cuts and bite marks disappeared in front of their eyes.

'Thank you so much, Skrinkle. My legs are back to normal, and not a cut in sight,' she said, and kissed the top of his head.

'You are most welcome! I was sent to keep you safe, after all,' he replied.

'I'm glad you're here, Skrinkle, but you could have pulled those pearl things out a bit sooner, and then I wouldn't have had to ruin my T-shirt,' laughed Ellis.

'Ah, humour, my boy! You know what, I like it,' chuckled Skrinkle.

Next, Skrinkle applied the pearls to Ellis's injured arm. Within seconds, the bite marks had vanished entirely. Ellis thanked Skrinkle.

Skrinkle closed the glass jar tight and placed it back in his coat pocket.

'We need to return to the cottage as quickly as possible. Otherwise, Mum and Dad will be freaking out. We've been gone too long!' said Lydia.

'Is it safe to leave?' Lydia asked Skrinkle.

'Perfectly safe, thanks to the Lauma. Remember what Zavantos told you? There is enchantment wherever you venture on earth.'

Skrinkle pressed his paw up against the inside of the tree trunk and called out, 'Goddess Lauma, please open if it is safe to do so.' The goddess's mouth began to open once more, and a large hole appeared again in the tree trunk, allowing Skrinkle, Lydia, and Ellis to walk out. Soon they were standing in front of the tree, looking at the goddess's face as she gently closed her mouth.

'Thank you, goddess Lauma, for keeping us safe. I will tell the mighty Zavantos of your kindness and courage when we return to Veena,' said Skrinkle.

'You are most welcome. The woods are enchanted, and will always protect you from the evil that is following you,' said an angelic voice. It was coming from the face in the tree. The face of the goddess looked to Lydia. 'They fear you, my child, because you are brave and determined in your quest to help Veena. No matter how dark it seems or however helpless you feel, you are stronger than you think.' The face smiled.

'I am truly grateful to you, goddess Lauma, for keeping my brother, my dearest friend Skrinkle, and me safe from the Sinaras. I had a dream once that evil creatures were chasing me through the woods. I guess you could say that my nightmare came true today,' replied Lydia.

'Don't fear the woods Lydia: there is much beauty to see in them. All you must do in your time of need is call out my name and all the woodland creatures, including the Woodilfs, will help you, my child.'

'They live in Gwendonia, in the dungeons,' Lydia told her excitedly.

'Yes, they do. They are protecting you and the castle, but you'll find them in the woods too,' Lauma smiled.

'Goddess Lauma, you have helped me yet again; I am forever in your debt.' Skrinkle bowed to the goddess.

'You are most welcome,' she replied, before the face disappeared into the bark of the tree until it could be seen no more.

They climbed down the tree roots and found themselves on the woodland floor.

'What's this huge mound of moss? It wasn't here when we were being chased by those creatures,' said Lydia.

The tree's roots looked as if they were grabbing at the carpet of moss; clutching it in long, outstretched fingers.

'You're right— how very observant of you, Lydia,' said Skrinkle. 'This moss is, in fact,' what's left of the Sinaras and the Mudum Lupus. The Lauma and the winged Esmaga destroyed them. Now and they will be rotting away in the woods for all eternity,' he smiled, before kicking and scattering the moss everywhere with his paws. 'Now, they're just like any other pile of moss you would see when walking in the woods.'

Ellis couldn't believe what had happened in the past hour; he was quiet and didn't speak, which was unusual for him as he was always talking and joking around. Lydia noticed how withdrawn her brother had become. 'Ellis,' are you OK?'

'I think so. 'It's all so weird.'

'I don't feel so alone now that I have you and Skrinkle by my side. We can't tell mum, or dad, or our grandparents— no one, Ellis. Understand?'

'I won't tell anyone, I promise. It'll be our secret,' he reassured her.

As they neared the entrance to the woods, Skrinkle spun around and transformed himself back into a fox cub. Lydia picked him up and popped him into her bag. Ellis was amazed. 'That's just so cool,' he giggled, while shaking his head.

'Thank you, Ellis, I aim to please,' said Skrinkle.

'Next time, you and your brother may want to take the transformation discs. The ones professor Quelldar gave you,' said Skrinkle.

'Yes, I was a little complacent, wasn't I? I thought we wouldn't need them; how wrong I was,' said Lydia.

'Next time, we'll be more prepared, and we will use the discs if required. You and Ellis were in real danger today,' said Skrinkle, shaking his head.

'Where do you think the remaining two Diamond Angels are, Skrinkle? Do you have any indication where they could be?' asked Ellis.

'If we knew that, my boy, there wouldn't be any need for this dangerous quest. Lady Ronan and her ancestors spent their lives trying to help us but to no avail, I'm afraid. We must continue the quest and search for clues to find the remaining two Diamond Angels. Wouldn't it just be wonderful to find them, so Veena could be one kingdom again and for Ballam to be destroyed once and for all,' said Skrinkle.

'Veena is the most wonderful of places. You'll love Uze the giant, the Tulwens, the Haflis, the Duons . . . oh and the Spellters and Lutin, who's very naughty but funny. You'll like him! Then there's the mighty Zavantos, leader of the Ogara dragons, who is guarding the Lamanya plinth,' Lydia gabbled. 'I didn't want to leave, did I Skrinkle?'

'That is true, Lydia,' he smiled.

'I'm sure to love Veena as much as you,' said Ellis, smiling.

Soon, they were nearing the safety of Adores cottage.

'I'm glad that we've made it home after that horrendous experience in the woods,' said Lydia.

'Yes, me too. Do you think we'll encounter any more of those creatures in Ireland, Skrinkle?' asked Ellis.

'I am not able to say, I'm afraid. We'll need to be vigilant. We need to keep together. I will try to keep you both safe.'

'Lydia, don't we have to visit those kids tomorrow?' asked Ellis, letting out the biggest of sighs.

'Yes, we do, I'm afraid.'

'I will have to come with you,' said Skrinkle. 'Just pop me in your bag like today.'

'You know what? I think that's a brilliant idea. You can keep a lookout and keep checking the Lamanya Stone,' said Lydia, noticing the confusion on her brother's face. 'The Lamanya Stone contains angels who move inside it when danger is near,' she explained.

'Oh, OK,' he replied, still looking bewildered.

'Then it's settled. I'll accompany you to Abban Manor tomorrow,' said Skrinkle.

Ellis was overwhelmed by what Skrinkle had told him about the annals of Veena and the callous and evil Ballam, and he couldn't stop thinking about the nightmarish Sinaras and their hideous pack of Mudum Lupus. Ellis knew then that he would continue to protect his sister on her quest to restore the realm of Veena.

Chapter 11

Abban Manor

The following day, Lydia and Ellis prepared for their visit to Abban Manor. They would have preferred to remain in the safety of Adores cottage, but how could they tell their grandparents and parents that they were afraid to leave the cottage for fear of running into evil Sinaras and snarling Mudum Lupus?

In her bedroom, Lydia, Ellis, and Skrinkle were talking about the events of the previous day. The children were relieved that Skrinkle would be accompanying them on their visit, as he would be able to alert them to any potential dangers that they may encounter on their way.

'I hope we can walk there and back without coming across any more of those Sinaras,' sighed Lydia.

'Yes, me too,' said Ellis.

'I'll protect you as much as I am able but, as I told you before, they could be absolutely anywhere, I'm afraid. 'I'll wait here till you've had your lunch and check that we have everything we might need in the bag,' said Skrinkle.

'We'll come and fetch you,' said Lydia, giving him a little smile before going downstairs.

Skrinkle began emptying the contents of her bag onto the bed and checked that everything was there. 'Diamond Angel, Golden Key, Lamanya Stone, bag of transformation discs check, Chocolate biscuits? Not required! A torch, hmmm might be useful, ah, and packet of batteries . . . shells and pebbles? Maybe for arts and crafts, but certainly not for our quest!'

Having completed the check he placed the contents back in the bag. All he could do was wait for Lydia and Ellis to collect him, and wonder if they would need any of the objects he'd packed at all.

In the kitchen, Lydia and Ellis greeted their parents and grandparents, who were sitting around the kitchen table, flicking

153

through a pile of photo albums. 'Come and see photos of you when you were small,' said their mother.

Lydia and Ellis sat down and began poring over the many photos strewn over the large kitchen table. As they reminisced there was much laughter along with a little sadness, especially when coming across photos of relatives who had passed on. Lydia loved rummaging through the old photographs. Ellis on the other hand, was initially interested in looking only at old photos of himself. However, his enthusiasm soon began to wane as he was 'starving' and eager to have lunch.

As Lydia looked through the photos, she came across an old, tattered photo album bound in black leather. She began looking at the black and white photos inside and noticed they were of her grandmother when she was a young girl and working at Abban Manor. 'Nanna, you were so pretty,' said Lydia.

'I was a bit of a looker, I suppose,' replied her grandmother, chuckling.

'She was the prettiest in all of Wexford County, Lydia, and she chose me,' said Granda, smiling.

'You were handsome yourself, James Kelly, and you too could have had your pick of the prettiest girls around,' replied her grandmother.

'I'm the luckiest man in all of Ireland: I got to spend my life with you,' Granda said, giving his wife a gentle kiss on her cheek.

Lydia and Ellis looked at one another and smiled, knowing that their grandparents had spent a lifetime together and were still very much devoted to one another.

While her parents, grandparents, and Ellis pottered around the kitchen preparing lunch, Lydia studied a photo of her grandmother standing outside Abban Manor. 'Nanna, who are all these people in this photo?

'Let me see . . . that's me, then this is . . . ' she began naming every person in the picture. 'Ah, look there is the late Lord Kavanagh. He was a little eccentric, but he was such a lovely person. Look, Lydia, you see him?' she said, pointing to a younger man, 'That's the current Lord Charles Kavanagh. He must have only been in his early twenties when this picture was taken, and such a lovely man, so he is.'

Who's he, Nanna?' Lydia asked, pointing to a man standing next to Charles Kavanagh.

'Oh, I can't remember his name; it's such a long time ago! He once was a great friend of Charles's. They met when they were young,' replied her grandmother. Lydia studied the face more closely. 'He looks so familiar, Nanna.' Where had she seen the face before?

'No, you wouldn't know him. One time, he was a regular visitor at the manor, but he and Charles had a falling out, I believe. Well, that was the talk at the manor at the time, and he hasn't visited for years and years.'

'Where was he from, Nanna?

'England, I believe. Not sure what part, mind.'

Lydia gazed at the photo, trying to remember.

'Lydia, please put the photo albums away, it's time for lunch,' said her grandmother, smiling.

Lydia nodded and placed the photo albums into a neat pile on the dresser.

During lunch, their grandmother told Lydia and Ellis that Mrs Tolsdale would be expecting them, and that they shouldn't be late. 'You both make sure you are on time.'

'We'll be on time, don't worry, Nanna,' said Ellis.

'You'd better go and wash your face before you leave. You need to look your best,' said their mother.

'I will, Mum,' replied Lydia.

'I've already washed, Mum. I don't need to wash again,' moaned Ellis.

'You can go and wash again. You are not going to leave this cottage with tomato sauce all over your mouth, do you understand?' said his mother sternly, as Ellis tried to lick the sauce from around his mouth with his tongue.

'Yuck! You look like a lizard trying to catch bugs,' Lydia laughed.

Their mother was not happy with Ellis and started to lose her patience. 'Ellis, just wash your face, for goodness' sake!'

Ellis knew not to joke around any further. Once they had finished eating, he and Lydia washed their faces then went to fetch Skrinkle.

'It's now or never,' said Lydia, exhaling loudly.

155

'Come on, let's go to Abban Manor and get it over and done with. We won't be there long,' replied Ellis.

Skrinkle quickly scuttled into Lydia's bag, and the three of them made their way downstairs to the front door. They heard a voice call out: it was their mother. 'Be careful and stay together!' 'We will!' they shouted, as they closed the front door. Finally, they were on their way to the manor.

They followed the woodland path and told Skrinkle about the strange events that had taken place while their grandmother had been working at the manor. 'What strange things? I can't deal with more strange things happening, especially after yesterday,' he said, shuddering.

'Nanna said there were lots of banging noises, but no one knew where the noises came from. Also, the late Lord Kavanagh was eccentric, so who knows what he was doing? Perhaps experiments?' said Lydia, widening her eyes to their full capacity to scare her brother.

'I'm sure there is a perfect explanation regarding the banging noises,' replied Skrinkle, trying to reassure them.

'I hope you're right. There has been enough danger and weirdness. Still, I'm not confident the three of us won't come across further trouble,' said Ellis, looking concerned.

'We need to be strong and keep together. We can do this. We must believe that we can restore Veena, otherwise what's the point in us risking our lives?' said Skrinkle.

Lydia and Ellis looked at each other and knew that Skrinkle was right: they had to have faith in themselves.

'Just think, Ellis, we'll be in New York soon. No more visiting Abban Manor,' grinned Lydia.

'I'm worried about Nanna and Granda. I really don't want to be leaving them, especially now after all that has happened,' he replied.

'Never fear, Ellis: your grandparents will be perfectly safe. The Sinaras are not interested in them. They don't even know where they live. They'll be looking out for us, make no mistake,' said Skrinkle.

'I think it was them who passed the cottage, so they might know where I live,' replied Lydia, concerned.

'If they knew we were at the cottage, don't you think we'd have known by now?' replied Skrinkle.

'Are you sure? Can you give me your word that when we leave for New York, no harm will come to them?' said Ellis.

'I give you my word,' replied Skrinkle.

'That's one less thing for us to worry about,' said Ellis, looking relieved.

'How far is the manor?' asked Skrinkle.

'About a mile, I think. It shouldn't take us too long to get there,' replied Ellis.

They came to a long, stone pathway, which eventually led them to the gates of the manor. In the distance, nestled among the woods, they could see the grand façade of Abban Manor. 'Doesn't it look lovely?' said Lydia enthusiastically.

'I suppose,' replied Ellis, who wasn't the slightest bit interested in the place.

'What about you, Skrinkle?' asked Lydia. There was no reply. 'Skrinkle? Skrinkle? Where are you?'

'I'm here, checking the Lamanya Stone! There appears to be some activity going on. You both keep walking, get to the manor as quickly as you can. Something is nearing us,' he replied.

Lydia and Ellis were scared by Skrinkle's news. They looked all around them.

'I can't see anything,' said Ellis, relieved.

'The Lamanya Stone is telling us there is evil and danger around,' Skrinkle warned them.

'Could it be to do with the manor? Could evil be there? See, I bet Nanna was right—strange things happened there,' said Lydia.

'Shh, both of you, I can hear people talking. Quickly, take cover behind the hedgerow,' Skrinkle demanded.

Lydia and Ellis made their way through a small gap in the hedgerow and sat on the grass. The only sounds they could hear were their own hearts pounding and the crows cawing in the skies above them. 'What are we going to do? We need to get to the manor on time. Otherwise, we'll be in big trouble,' said Lydia.

'Keep down and remain close to the hedgerow. We'll keep off the stone path and creep to the manor through the field,' said Skrinkle, looking worried.

As they crept along the hedge, the voices became louder and louder. 'Be deadly quiet. Something's not right,' said Skrinkle.

'I can't cope with seeing any more of those creatures,' cried Ellis, burying his head in his hands.

'Just keep calm, Ellis, please,' begged Lydia.

'I am calm. Those voices are *them*: I just know it,' he replied, clinging onto Lydia's bag.

Skrinkle peered through a tiny gap in the hedgerow to where the voices could be heard.

A small group of men and women were talking while sitting inside a dilapidated old stone barn. The gathering was their worst fear come true: Sinaras. They were talking about Ballam and that two of his servants had gone missing.

'How many of them are there?' whispered Lydia.

Ellis knelt and peeped through the small gap in the hedgerow. 'Five, six . . . there's seven of them. It was bad enough when there were two of them after us, but seven! We'll be lucky to stay alive if they catch us. We'll never get past them. They'll see us walking towards the manor.' Ellis looked at Skrinkle and Lydia, not knowing what to do.

Suddenly, they heard the same ghastly chant they had heard the day before. The Sinaras had formed a circle while holding hands. Lydia, Ellis, and Skrinkle watched as the Sinaras' faces began changing from human to the ugliest, scariest, and most grotesque creatures imaginable.

'We're going to die! We are not going to be able to get to the manor,' Ellis whimpered.

'What are we going to do, Skrinkle?' asked Lydia.

'You both need to be quiet. I need to think. They have the most impeccable hearing,' Skrinkle replied before disappearing inside Lydia's bag.

'Oh great, you just hide! Me and Lydia will sit behind the hedge and wait for them to catch and kill us,' said Ellis sarcastically.

'What's he doing? Why is he hiding in the bag?' asked Lydia.

Ellis could hear the Sinaras' conversation. 'Shh! They're talking about Skrinkle.'

One of the male Sinaras was talking. 'We'll need to look out for that interfering fox and anyone who is helping him. We'll go into the woods, capture the Woodilfs and torture them until they tell us where our friends are. Whoever it is helping Veena will live to regret it. We will destroy them all.' The Sinaras were all laughing hysterically and soon began chanting Ballam's name over and over.

Suddenly, there was silence. 'Lydia, I can't hear them chanting or speaking,' Ellis whispered. They summoned the courage to peek through the tiny gap in the hedge, hoping that the Sinaras had left.

'They're still there. They're not moving,' said Lydia,' her heart pounding rapidly.

'They've heard us. I'm positive they have,' said Ellis, not able to take his eyes off the Sinaras. 'One of them is walking towards the hedge. Look, Lydia! You'll need to run as fast as you can towards the manor. It's your only chance. I'll run in the opposite direction. Hopefully, they'll chase me and not you,' said Ellis, with tears in his eyes.

'I can't, I'm not leaving you,' said Lydia. She was crying too.

'I'm your big brother and you've got to listen to me. It's the rules. You're the best sister ever, and I love you,' he said, hugging her.

'I love you too. I'm sorry for being bossy and for all the mean things I've said to you. You're the best brother in the world,' she cried.

'When I say run, you must run— understand?' Lydia nodded while wiping away her tears.

Skrinkle reappeared. 'Not so quick—take one of these. I will also be taking one, as they are looking out for a fox,' said Skrinkle, clutching the bag containing the transformation discs.

'Professor Quelldar gave me these—they should protect us, Ellis,' said Lydia.

'We have no time to discuss the ins and outs. Pop them into your mouths immediately. The male Sinara is called Skelan and he is just as evil as his master, Ballam,' said Skrinkle shuddering.

As soon as the three of them had taken the Eralda Chartum transformation discs they instantly turned into Irish hares.

'We're rabbits! Why couldn't I have transformed into a stag? An animal that's powerful,' said Ellis.

'We're hares. We're harder to spot and we'll be at the manor in no time at all, without the Sinaras suspecting a thing,' said Skrinkle confidently.

'I can't believe I'm a rabbit! Those discs actually work. We're rabbits, Ellis,' said Lydia excitedly and admiring her bushy tail.

'Irish hares, not rabbits, Lydia,' said Skrinkle, shaking his head.

As the three of them sat on the grass, they felt an overwhelming urge to look up. Right above them was one of the female Sinaras, hovering in the air and looking down at them. She was a terrifying sight; her long, straight, black hair gently blowing in the breeze. Her black, soulless eyes, glaring out of her bony, milky-white face, bored into them. It felt as though they were once again experiencing the most horrifying of all nightmares. They were petrified and couldn't run, so they pretended to nibble on the grass.

'Do you see anything?' called out Skelan, who was still inside the barn.

'No, nothing of importance—just some mangy rabbits,' she shouted back.

'That's the sound we must have heard,' replied Skelan.

'Mmm maybe, but I'm not sure. Shall I catch them? They're probably edible,' said the female Sinara, who was still hovering above Lydia, Ellis, and Skrinkle.

'Best not. We have plenty to eat. Leave them. We need to be on our way and report back to Ballam,' he told her. With that, the female Sinaras flew over the hedge.

'We need to run across this field as fast as we can,' whispered Skrinkle. 'Ready? Go!'

Skrinkle, Lydia, and Ellis bounded across the field until finally they were out of sight. When they were no longer in danger, they transformed back into their true selves.

'I can't believe it! We were hares, running across the field!' gasped Lydia.

'It was mad, wasn't it?' said Ellis excitedly.

'That was a close call. I thought they were going to take us,' said Skrinkle.

'Yes, me too, but the discs saved us,' said Lydia.

'They most certainly did,'' beamed Skrinkle.

'Where do you suppose the Sinaras are going? Where do they live?' Lydia asked Skrinkle.

Skrinkle was keeping watch. 'I haven't the faintest idea. They are, after all, Odium Morphs.'

'Oh no, what if they capture the Woodilfs? We must tell the goddess Lauma,' said Lydia.

'Don't worry about the Woodilfs; they'll be perfectly safe. Goddess Lauma and the woodland creatures will kill the Sinaras if they dare venture into the enchanted woods. That I can assure you.'

They walked along a long grit path that led to the iron gates of Abban Manor. 'We finally made it,' said Lydia.

'Look at the sign: it says trespassers will be prosecuted. We can't go in,' said Ellis.

'But we're not trespassers, are we? The Kavanaghs know we are coming to visit, and we'll make ourselves known by knocking on the door,' said Lydia.

'We don't know these people. I don't know why Nanna made us come here. We're going to be walking on their property. What if they have ferocious dogs? They'll maul us,' said Ellis.

Lydia paused for a moment, thinking that Ellis might be right. However, she soon dismissed the thought. 'I can't hear any dogs barking, and I'm sure that if they had dogs, they would have sniffed us out by now.' She opened one of the enormous iron gates. 'Come on, let's walk up to the house.'

'Not another long path! Never mind, we'll be in New York soon, and those creepy things won't find us there,' said Ellis.

'Do you not understand Ellis? The Sinaras are everywhere on this earth plane, walking among us. I'm afraid we are not safe, even in New York. The only time we'll be safe is once Veena is restored and Ballam and his servants are destroyed,' said Skrinkle.

'Yes, I understand,' Ellis replied sullenly.

'Skrinkle, you must hide; you can't be seen. We're nearly at the manor,' said Lydia.

Quickly, he buried himself under the contents of Lydia's bag and kept quiet.

Abban Manor was a grand-looking Georgian-style building, with lots of square windows and an imposing wooden front door with the most elaborate cast-iron doorknocker in the shape of a gargoyle. When Lydia saw the gargoyle she smiled, as it reminded her of the Groylers, Lutin, and Yogan. She desperately wanted to return to Veena and to Gwendonia.

'You can knock the door! I'm not touching that creepy thing. I'll stand behind you,' said Ellis, taking two steps back.

'For goodness' sake, we've been chased by evil and you're moaning about touching a gargoyle doorknocker,' huffed Lydia.

'Just knock on the door please, I can't wait to get home,' said Ellis, looking all around.

Lydia lifted the heavy doorknocker and banged it hard against the oak door. *Thud! Thud! Thud!* She glanced up casually at the large crest above the doorway, and saw *1776* chiselled in the stonework.

'That's the same date as the one I saw at Gwendonia and at Rubbelswick Chambers,' said Lydia.

As they waited for the door to open, Lydia looked around the pristine gardens and ornamental fountain, which had dozens of cherubs carved into its stonework. 'Ellis, look. They're the same cherubs as you see at Gwendonia—the Asiras,' she murmured.

Ellis looked at the fountain. 'They do look a lot like the ones at Gwendonia,' he agreed.

'Ellis, it's the same date too: 1776, just like the carving in Lady Ronan's bedroom. There must be another one here; there just has to be,' she babbled. 'It's way too much of a coincidence, Ellis, don't you think?'

'What are you talking about, Lydia?' he asked.

'The other doorway; another Diamond Angel,' she said.

'I don't think so. Let's just meet these kids and get home as soon as we can,' he replied.

Lydia wondered if it was just a coincidence. However, she felt wholeheartedly that Abban Manor was hiding secrets, which would hopefully lead to a link between the house and the realm of Veena. Lydia's thoughts were interrupted when she heard footsteps approaching the front door.

The heavy oak door opened to reveal a tall, smiling, middle-aged woman. Her greying hair was pulled back into a tight bun that sat on top of her head.

'Welcome, Lydia, Ellis,' the woman said in a strong Irish accent, 'I'm Mrs Tolsdale, housekeeper of Abban Manor and long-time friend of your grandmother Bridget. Please come in,' she beamed.

Lydia and Ellis walked into the hallway of the manor, passing Mrs Tolsdale. 'Thank you, Mrs Tolsdale, for inviting us,' they both said politely.

'You're welcome,' she responded, before directing them into the drawing room and bustling off to fetch the Kavanagh children.

The drawing room overlooked the front gardens; Lydia and Ellis could see the ornamental fountain and its waters spraying high into the air.

Lydia's thoughts went back to the carved fountain. 'It's lovely, but the cherubs remind me so much of Gwendonia, Ellis. I miss Grandad and Gran and the castle. I wish Nanna and Granda also lived with us at the castle, but their home is in Ireland,' said Lydia.

'When we return from visiting Aunt Evie and Uncle Steven, they'll be coming to stay at Gwendonia,' said Ellis.

'Yes, you're right. It'll be nice to have the family finally back together,' she smiled.

While they waited patiently for the Kavanagh children, Lydia asked Skrinkle if he was all right, as he'd been nestled away in her bag for a while.

'I'm fine, don't worry about me,' he replied.

'I wish those kids would hurry up! Who do they think they are, making us wait for them?' muttered Ellis.

Ellis did not know how he should behave in front of the Kavanaghs and was feeling uneasy. Would they have anything in common? Ellis was proud of his family and upbringing and didn't want it snotty-nosed posh kids looking down on him.

Just as Ellis finished whingeing about how long they'd been waiting, the door of the drawing-room opened and in walked Mrs Tolsdale along with Phineas, Verity, and Ophelia Kavanagh.

Lydia walked towards the children. 'Hello, I'm Lydia and this is my brother, Ellis. We saw you when we were at the beach,' said Lydia.

'Yes, we saw you: looked like you were having fun,' said Phineas.

'Yes, we were,' replied Ellis, walking towards Lydia and standing next to her. 'We were told by our grandmother to come and introduce ourselves. She worked in this house for many years, and said that she knew you and your parents. So here we are, it was so lovely meeting the three of you, but we must go now,' said Ellis.

'But you've only just got here! You wish to leave already? That's so awfully rude,' said Verity.

'Nothing rude about it. I don't think you want me and my sister here anyway, so we'll leave you to get on with whatever you were doing before we knocked on the door, where you made us wait for you for fifteen minutes. That qualifies as rude, wouldn't you say?' said Ellis. 'Come on, Lydia, we're leaving.'

'Ellis, please don't leave. I want to stay and get to know them,' said Lydia.

'Look, we're so sorry that we made you wait, but we were in the middle of something that we just couldn't leave,' replied Phineas.

Ophelia noticed the tense atmosphere between them all. 'Shall we start over again?' she said, smiling, while Verity and Phineas stood poker-faced. Phineas was a tall boy with brown hair, light-green eyes, and was around the same age as Ellis. Kind-natured Ophelia had waist-length blonde hair and piercing blue eyes, while Verity appeared to be opinionated, entitled, and a madam, with long, ginger hair and blue eyes.

After an awkward silence, the five of them began to chat. 'We have to feed our horses. Would you like to help us?' asked Phineas.

'Yes, we would love to. We love horses, don't we, Ellis? How many horses do you have?' asked Lydia.

'We have eight horses, two cats, and a guinea pig named Oink,' said Verity, giggling. The five of them made their way outside to the stables, along with Skrinkle, who had remained remarkably quiet inside Lydia's bag. Soon, they were all happily feeding the horses until Verity started shouting at Ophelia and Phineas. 'Where are the cats? Where are they?' she demanded.

'Will you shut up moaning all the time? They're around here somewhere,' replied Phineas.

'Don't tell me to shut up! *You* shut up!' she yelled back at Phineas.

Ophelia screamed at the top of her voice, 'Will you two just stop arguing!' She stamped her foot and there was silence. Lydia, Ellis, Phineas, and Verity looked at Ophelia and they all burst out laughing.

'I wasn't expecting that. It's like when Ellis and me argue,' Lydia said.

'Yeah, she always shouts at me,' said Ellis, smiling.

Their laughter soon stopped when they saw two jet-black cats walking towards them. They were identical to Lady Ronan's cats. 'There you are,' gushed Verity.

Lydia could not take her eyes off the cats. Ellis looked at his sister, knowing exactly what she was thinking: the cherubs, the date on the crest, and now the two black cats. They all pointed to Gwendonia Castle.

Lydia turned around, opened her bag, and began whispering to Skrinkle about the similarities.

Verity noticed. 'What on earth are you doing, talking into your bag? You look absolutely mad.'

'She's not mad, so keep your nose out! You're horrible. You're nothing like your brother and sister,' said Ellis, fuming.

'Verity, can you just for once stop being yourself and at least try to be nice,' said Ophelia.

'I am lovely. She just looks insane, talking into her bag,' Verity replied.

Ellis became agitated. 'I won't tell you again, stop calling my sister mad. She isn't mad, do you understand? You don't know anything at all.'

Lydia didn't care what Verity was saying about her, however: she just continued whispering to Skrinkle.

'You've got something in your bag that's moving!' screamed Verity.

'What are you screaming for?' asked Phineas.

'Her bag, it's moving. She has something in there,' said Verity, pointing and waving her finger.

'You're such a drama queen, Verity. What if Lydia has something in her bag? It's nothing to do with you,' said Ophelia. Lydia turned around, clutching her bag, and looked directly at her brother. She was frozen to the spot and couldn't speak.

'What's wrong with you?' asked Ellis.

'Are you OK, Lydia?' asked Ophelia.

Verity and Phineas looked at one another, baffled by Lydia's demeanour.

Lydia began whispering into her brother's ear, while the Kavanagh children looked on, trying desperately to hear what she was saying. Lydia composed herself and asked the children if she and Ellis could hide in the stables for a while.

'Why on earth do you want to hide in our stables? said Verity.

Lydia and Ellis dismissed Verity's question.

'Yes, of course you can use the stables,' replied Phineas.

'Thank you, Phineas,' replied Lydia, who then turned and ran with Ellis into the stables and huddled together behind several large bales of hay. The Kavanagh children followed them and found Lydia and Ellis looking terrified.

'What's wrong with you two? Is there anything we can do?' asked Ophelia, while Verity looked on, finding the whole thing totally bizarre.

Ellis begged for them to be quiet and told them they needed to hide.

'Hide? Why should we hide? Hide from what?' said Verity defiantly.

'Please be quiet and I promise we'll explain!' pleaded Lydia.

Shrugging, Phineas joined Lydia behind the hay bales, and Verity and Ophelia followed.

'It's time you met our special friend,' she told them.

'What do you mean?' said Verity, her arms folded.

'Will you just be quiet for a minute,' replied Lydia.

Lydia placed her bag on the floor next to her feet and gently put both hands into her bag before picking up Skrinkle, holding him close to her.

Ophelia gushed. 'Aww, it's a little fox cub.'

'It's ever so cute. Can I have a hold?' asked Ophelia.

'I'm sorry I called you mad, Lydia,' said Verity.

'Are you saying sorry to Lydia, Verity?' smirked Phineas.

166

'Well, what if I am?' she replied.

'I accept your apology, Verity,' said Lydia, still looking scared.

'There's something we need to tell you,' said Ellis.

The Kavanagh children looked at one another, confused. 'What are you talking about?' asked Phineas.

'Please don't be scared or freaked out! You have nothing to be frightened of,' Lydia reassured them. Lydia's comment, unfortunately, only heightened the children's anxiety further.

Verity thought perhaps that Lydia was a little mad after all, and felt that she had apologised to her too soon. Lydia began whispering into Skrinkle's ear, while Ellis watched the looks on the Kavanagh children's faces. He knew exactly what was going to happen next.

'You see, this fox cub, he's our special friend,' said Lydia.

'That's lovely, but what's so special about that? Even though it's cute, it's just a baby fox. Nothing to be frightened of, is there?' said Verity, sounding bored and rolling her eyes.

At that moment, Skrinkle transformed into an adult fox. Phineas, Ophelia, and Verity stood in shock, their mouths wide open, and rubbing their eyes.

Ellis looked at the Kavanagh children. 'Not so mad now, is she?'

Skrinkle retold the story of Veena, just had he'd done with Lydia and Ellis, to the Kavanagh children. They hung onto every word, fascinated.

Lydia and Ellis told them all about the evil Sinaras being in Wexford Town and the horrifying encounters that had taken place in the enchanted woods, and of their latest encounter with the Sinaras on their way to Abban Manor.

'The Lamanya Stone angels are moving. We need to hide,' said Skrinkle. The Kavanaghs didn't question him, and sat down beside Lydia and Ellis.

Skrinkle peeked out from behind the hay bales and began creeping towards the entrance of the stables.

'Be careful, Skrinkle,' whispered Lydia, while Ellis, Phineas, Verity, and Ophelia sat quietly, unsure of what to say or do, and petrified.

As Skrinkle looked out towards the manor, he saw four men and women lurking by the front door. He scuttled back to where they were sat quietly. 'Quickly, Lydia, check the Lamanya Stone. Four people are standing outside the door,' he told them.

'The angels are moving, Skrinkle, they are still warning us,' she replied.

'What if it's the same people we saw at the beach, Lydia?' said Ellis, panicking.

Phineas told them that he had also seen four adults at the beach. Without hesitation, he darted to the entrance of the stables to see if they were the same people that he had seen. 'It's them! I remember what they were wearing,' he said. 'What are we going to do?'

'They're not looking for you, Phineas, or your sisters. They are looking for Lydia, Ellis and, of course, me. You should be safe,' said Skrinkle.

'What do you mean, *should be*?' whispered Verity through gritted teeth.

'There's always the Eralda Chartum. I suppose we could take those.'

Lydia rummaged into her bag and pulled out the transformation discs, placing them into the palm of her hand.

'We only took one an hour ago and we were transformed into Irish hares,' said Ellis.

'It doesn't matter how many times you take them. When your life is in danger you must eat one—it's as simple as that, Ellis,' said Skrinkle.

'Do you mean if we eat one of those black things, we'll transform into an animal?' giggled Verity, not believing a word.

'Look, Verity, how many three-foot talking foxes have you come across, apart from me? None I would guess,' Skrinkle spluttered. 'What I am saying is the truth. I come from an enchanted world named Veena. I've been sent here to protect Lydia, do you understand?'

'Listen to Skrinkle. He is wise and will always protect us and he would never harm us,' Lydia reassured her new friends.

'Someone is coming. I can hear footsteps walking towards the stables,' said Ellis, sounding terrified.

Lydia opened her palm of her hand, revealing the small, round black discs.

'It's time for us to take them—quickly pop them into your mouths,' she ordered. Lydia, Skrinkle, Ellis, Phineas, and Ophelia immediately placed them on their tongues and instantly they transformed into black thoroughbred horses. Verity, who still hadn't taken her disc, looked shocked and couldn't move. Suddenly the stable door flew open, and in walked the four strangers. They moved furtively around the stables. Verity could see them from where she was hiding. As they slowly walked towards where she was sitting, she placed the disc on her tongue and transformed into a piglet and began running around the stables, oinking and squealing, furious she hadn't transformed into a thoroughbred horse like her siblings. She careered out of the stables, nearly knocking over one of the strangers. Lydia, Skrinkle, Ellis, Phineas, and Ophelia raised their noses in the air and curled their upper lips back as if they were laughing at Verity being transformed into a piglet.

The strangers continued to search the stables. Skrinkle knew instantly they were the Sinaras, even without them transforming into hideous creatures. And he knew that they were searching for him, Lydia, and Ellis. The Sinaras, however, didn't know that they were looking at the very people they wanted, because they didn't know about the enchanted transformation discs.

Verity was still running around the grounds of the manor, squealing. The Sinaras approached Lydia, Skrinkle, Ellis, Phineas, and Ophelia, in their thoroughbred horse disguises.

'Why do these four-legged creatures appear to be smiling at us?' one of the female Sinaras said, menacingly.

'What are you talking about? Horse creatures don't smile, you fool,' replied one of the male Sinaras.

'How dare you speak to me like that? Do you know I could kill you instantly?' she replied angrily. She walked up to the male Sinara, her eyes widening, and gave him the evilest of stares before gripping him by his throat with a veiny hand and digging her long, bony fingers into his neck.

'One squeeze and I could end your life, you FOOL!' she warned, and let out a baleful laugh.

'I'm sorry, Vana,' the male Sinara cringed, before falling to the ground, where he coughed and gasped, trying to catch his breath.

'Come, we need to leave. There is nothing here for us. The place is empty apart from these four-legged beasts,' said Vana, who appeared to be in charge. They left the stables, and swept past the manor house. Skrinkle was hoping that they wouldn't return. After ten minutes they all transformed back into themselves. Lydia rushed to check the Lamanya Stone: it was peaceful.

'We're safe—they've gone,' she told them, feeling relieved.

'I'm going to look for Verity,' said Phineas, running out of the stables.

'We'll talk when you return with your sister!' Skrinkle shouted after him. Ophelia sat holding onto her knees with both hands and was shaking with fear.

'Ophelia, are you OK?' asked Lydia.

'I was a horse! Then those evil things, what are they called again?'

'Sinaras,' replied Ellis.

'We know what you are feeling and going through,' Lydia reassured her.

'My sister is a piglet! She transformed into a piglet,' said Ophelia, while laughing hysterically and Lydia, Skrinkle, and Ellis began quietly chuckling along with her.

'I've found her!' shouted Phineas, and he appeared with his sister in the stables.

'Where were you, Verity? You're soaking wet,' Ophelia asked.

'Go on, tell them where I found you,' smirked Phineas.

'I'm not talking to any of you ever again,' she pouted.

'Where did you find her, Phineas?' asked Ophelia, while Lydia, Skrinkle, and Ellis looked on expectantly.

'She was hiding in the orchard, having been sprayed with pesticide,' said Phineas, who was chewing the inside of his cheek to stop himself laughing. The others looked at Verity with amusement.

'Go on, laugh, I don't care! I was petrified being a pig while you lot were horses. What was that about?' she shouted. 'And I ran past those strangers while trying to hide, so I headed for the orchards. That's when I got sprayed!' she yelled. Phineas and

Ophelia burst out laughing.

'We're sorry for laughing, but a piglet and pesticide all in one day,' they chuckled. Lydia, Skrinkle, and Ellis just grinned, trying to be polite.

Verity was furious with her siblings for making fun of her, but calmed down as they sat to
talk about the seriousness of their encounter with the Sinaras.

'Sinaras, here at Abban Manor? Don't be so ridiculous! We have nothing to do with them, or their master Ballsom,' said Verity.

'Verity, the strangers you saw in the stables were the Sinaras, and his name is Ballam, not Ballsom,' replied Skrinkle, looking concerned.

Verity said nothing.

'You should have seen Vana. She was ruthless—she was the one in charge of the group of Sinaras,' Phineas told Verity.

Verity was told every detail of what had happened inside the stables. Skrinkle reminded her, 'If they find out you so much as spoke one word with us, you will perish along with your siblings. Do you understand the seriousness of it, Verity?'

'They are looking for you, not us,' she replied.

'That is true. But what if any of the Sinaras saw us walking towards Abban Manor, just like the four Sinaras, with whom we had the unfortunate encounter earlier? Our lives were in extreme danger. You and your siblings were in danger too,' continued Skrinkle.

Phineas suggested they all go to the old stone barn, where the Sinaras had been earlier. 'We could look for clues; see where they were hiding.'

After a long discussion, it was decided that they would all make their way back to barn.

Skrinkle was hoping that the Sinaras had left some clues behind that would warn them of their whereabouts or their mission.

When they arrived, Ellis, Lydia, and Skrinkle walked in first, followed by the Kavanagh children. Once inside, Skrinkle gave the orders. 'Ellis and Lydia, you go to the first floor, and I'll remain on the ground floor with the others.'

Lydia and Ellis climbed up the rickety wooden steps and

immediately began looking for clues. Lydia scanned the floor but couldn't find anything.

'Come here, Lydia!' shouted Ellis. She rushed to where her brother was standing. In the corner of the room there were huge clumps of fox fur and piles of animal bones.

'Ellis, we can't tell Skrinkle, it's so sad.'

'Can't tell me what, Lydia?' he asked.

Lydia and Ellis didn't want Skrinkle to see the pile of fox fur and bones and encouraged him to look for Phineas.

'I know what you're trying to do. You are trying to protect me from seeing the fur and bones piled up in the corner. This is what the Sinaras do—they kill all innocent foxes looking for me.' He turned and descended the wooden steps, and Lydia and Ellis quickly followed him.

They all continued searching the ground floor. Suddenly, Ellis began screaming and holding his leg in agony. Skrinkle and Lydia ran to where Ellis was lying. He was writhing in pain. 'What happened Ellis?' said Lydia, who was concerned for her brother.

'Something bit me, Lydia,' he replied in a breathless voice. Ophelia shouted and pointed. 'Look, there's a weasel climbing up the wall!'

'I knew it!' shouted Skrinkle, as he began chasing the weasel around the barn. Skrinkle was extremely fast and gripped it with his claws, killing it instantly.

'What if there are more of them in the barn?' asked Lydia, sounding worried.

'If there were more Addanacs, we would have seen them,' replied Skrinkle.

'Addanacs? They're just weasels, Skrinkle,' said Lydia.

'They may look a lot like your weasels on the earth plane, but they belong to Ballam. This one has poisoned your brother,' said Skrinkle, pointing to the lifeless carcass.

'Quickly, check the Lamanya Stone, Lydia,' Skrinkle urged.

'It's moving! What are we going to do?' asked Lydia.

'Phineas, Verity, and Ophelia—run as fast as you can. You must not come back to look for us, do you understand?' he told them.

'We can't leave the three of you here,' Phineas replied.

'You must! Your lives are in danger! Now go.'

Reluctantly, the Kavanagh children ran form the barn.

'Get up, Ellis, please,' sobbed Lydia. 'Do something, Skrinkle, please. Don't let anything happen to him,' she begged.

'We must hide, Lydia, someone is coming.'

'We can't leave him! What are you thinking, Skrinkle?'

'We are not leaving him,' he replied.

Lydia and Skrinkle hid, not letting Ellis out of their sight.

'It's a woman, I can see her,' said Lydia.

As the woman walked near to where Ellis was lying Lydia gasped. 'I know her! She can help us! It's Mrs Sinclare from St Cein's Church,' she said, feeling relived.

'Don't make yourself known, Lydia,' warned Skrinkle.

'Whatever do you mean? She's such a lovely lady.

'Just look at the Lamanya Stone—I bet there is still movement, still warning us, Lydia.'

Lydia gazed at the Lamanya Stone, and the angels inside were moving, warning them against evil and danger.

Mrs Sinclare began talking to Ellis. 'What are you doing here? Are you OK? It's me, Mrs Sinclare, from the church,' she continued.

'Oh, Mrs Sinclare, I'm so pleased to see you! Can you help me get back to my grandparents? I was bitten by something,' said Ellis, who was drifting in and out of consciousness.

'Where's Lydia, Ellis?' she asked eagerly. 'Where is she? Tell me where she is?'

'Why do you want to know where my sister is?' he replied. 'Can you please help me, Mrs Sinclare?' Ellis pleaded.

'If you help me and tell me where your sister is, I'll help you. It's as simple as that, Ellis,' she replied menacingly.

'I don't know where she is!'

'Oh, you must do better than that, Ellis.'

'Why won't you help me?'

'Because you're not helping ME!' she screamed at him.

Ellis could not respond to Mrs Sinclare, as he was now unconscious. However, Lydia knew that this was not Mrs Sinclare, the lovely, kind woman who worked at St Cein's Church: she had turned into the most grotesque Sinara and was now letting out the deadliest of screams.

173

Lydia was shaking with fright and couldn't comprehend what she was seeing. 'Mrs Sinclare, the woman from the church—she's a Sinara, Skrinkle!' she whimpered in shock. She stared at her brother, knowing his life was in imminent danger.

How would Lydia and Skrinkle be able to save Ellis from the clutches of Mrs Sinclare? Would there be more Sinaras joining her in the barn? And would this be the day that Lydia would finally come face to face with Ballam? The nightmare had only just begun.

Made in the USA
Monee, IL
13 March 2022

92811879R00098